A Fear of Heights

A Fear of Heights

Virginia Coffman

This edition first published in
Great Britain in 1991 by
Judy Piatkus (Publishers) Ltd of
5 Windmill Street, London W1

British Library Cataloguing in Publication Data
Coffman, Virginia *1914–*
A Fear of Heights.
I. Title
813.54 [F]

ISBN 0–7499–0059–8

Printed and bound in Great Britain by
Billing & Sons Ltd, Worcester

WITH LOVE TO JO AND HARRY NORWOOD WHO SHARE OUR AFFECTION FOR OUR NATIVE CITY BY THE GOLDEN GATE

CHAPTER 1

I was nervous, and I was early for that all-important first meeting; so I stood outside the St. Francis Hotel, just beyond the entrance canopy, and tried to concentrate on the cable car grinding and clanging its way up the Powell Street hill "crowded to the gills," as Father used to say.

. . . *Father used to say* . . .

It was impossible to get my mind off the subject of my father and his re-entrance into my life after twenty years. Even now it seemed miraculous. My spur of the moment ad in the *Personals* column of several West Coast papers had produced this enormous dividend: the father I last saw at the age of five when Mother gave up trying to "civilize" her longshoreman-seafaring husband and divorced him on some fancied cause, returning to the well-cushioned bosom of her family in Chicago.

Now, twenty years later, Thomas Michael Tracey, having satisfied my investigators of his identity, asked to meet me in the spacious, red-carpeted new lobby of the St. Francis where I came to stay after I heard the good news that Father was very much alive and willing to see me. But the closer the hour of that meeting approached the more I began to doubt.

I recalled the maddening cynicism of Adam McKendrick, the investigator I had hired. Even after my father was located, Adam—that is, Mr. McKendrick—stubbornly insisted on reminding me of a fact with which I was perfectly familiar: my inheritance from my mother—herself the sole heir to the estates of her parents and her grandmother—was considerable, invested chiefly in industrial and Chicago high-rise properties, with a more than generous monthly trust income to me from blue chip stocks and municipal and state bonds from all over the country. If I died now, by accident, illness or otherwise, anyone claiming to be Thomas Michael Tracey might be in line to inherit over four million dollars. It might be a sobering thought, but it was not Adam McKendrick's business to tell me so.

The cable car made it to the top of the hill and ground to a halt on California Street, with human beings hanging on at every conceivable angle. The way Father used to hang on, so he could leap off in front of our old Victorian-gingerbread house on the less "Nabob" side of Nob Hill.

. . . *What has he been doing all these years? How has he lived? Did he marry again? Children! Good heavens! Maybe I've got some half-brothers and sisters. I'd like that.*

Being the daughter of a socially minded mother, I had long ago learned to rely upon myself for "good company." I had boyfriends in Chicago. No lovers, but several males of assorted ages who made ideal companions at the restaurant, the theater, or on the tennis court. I worked as a secretary in the law firm founded by my great-grandfather and presently run by Mother's friend, Glenn Rivercombe, and until I got this marvelous idea of locating Father, my chief pleasure had been in yearly cruises to Europe. It was amazing what an education one still acquired on shipboard, providing one was careful to undertake only the chase, not the capture.

But when the idea of locating Father came to me, hardly a year after my absentee-mother's death in her speeding Porsche, it seemed as if a whole new, warm and comforting world opened up before me. I was no longer alone. Somewhere in the world, probably on the Pacific Coast, there might still be someone to whom I belonged. My father.

I was shaken out of my thoughts and uncertainties by the voices of two hippies behind me, excitedly looking for the next cable car: "Hyde Street, Man! That's the one coming. Stops by the Buena Vista! And, Christ, it's six P.M. We'll waste the whole night!"

Six o'clock! I turned and hurried back under the canopy, up the broad steps and into the hotel lobby. Perhaps Thomas Michael Tracey was already here among the groups milling about the popular San Francisco meeting place. It depressed me to realize that I might not even recognize him after twenty years.

As a child I had been very fond of him. He may not have been a very good provider, but he always had time to charm his small daughter, to take her on fascinating walks up and down the hills of the city, to buy her sodas, to be, in short, the perfect father to a child who recognized early that her conception was an accident much regretted by her mother.

Adam McKendrick had offered to be present at my meeting with Father, as if I needed protection, but I had refused, somewhat indignantly. From the first Mr. McKendrick had been a disappointment as a "private eye." He was tall, blue-eyed, sandy-haired, rather obnoxiously unmarried and undoubtedly well endowed in every way that money and inherited graces could provide. He did not resemble Humphrey Bogart in the least. He was not even mysterious, and worst of all, he was vouched for as respectable by my own Chicago legal firm.

Then I saw Father come loping along the full length of the huge lobby, his hard, weathered, humorous Irish face hardly changed from the way it had looked in my childhood. He might almost have posed for the portrait of Tom Tracey that remained fixed in my memory over all the years. He hadn't gained much weight. His shoulders weren't quite as square. He stooped a trifle, but that wasn't too surprising, and I had expected the tousled gray hair which was grizzled, thinning, but far from gone.

I wanted to run toward him but found myself absolutely rigid with tension. Not fear, surely! Anyway, Father obviously didn't have the same uncertainty. He never had! He came on, directly toward me. It was clear someone, probably McKendrick, had showed him a picture of me.

Across several groups of people he called: "Hi, Sprout!" exactly like the old days.

He was Father. He must be. I had pictured myself holding out my hands, being friendly but dignified. It was no use. He reached me, gave me a big bear hug that lifted me an inch or two off the thick carpet, and all my good resolutions were gone. I hugged him exactly as I had when I was five.

"Barbara-Jane, my little girl!"

"Oh, Dad! It's been such a long time!"

"Yeah, Honey. Like the fella says—'long time no . . .' "

"No quotes, Dad. Remember?"

He grinned. "Your maw—your mother hated 'em. Said I had a lousy vocabulary. She never did make a gent out of me. Just couldn't rub the South-a-Marketer out of me, I reckon."

We started to walk with our arms interlocked. I hadn't been able to reach around him in the old days.

"Hey," he said, "let's go somewhere and talk. Tell me all about my little girl. My colleen's grown into a real black-Irish beauty. How'd you do it, with a dad looking like me, and a mother that—" He caught himself but I laughed.

"How about going up to the cocktail bar on top of the hotel's new tower? So long as we take the inside elevators," I added, pretending to laugh at an old fear of mine. "Here are the elevators, on the right."

"You old enough to drink, Sprout? You sure date me. Know that?"

As I looked at him, I said truthfully, "You never date. You're just like you were when . . . a long time ago."

The relationship, almost astonishingly, seemed to pick up where it had been broken off twenty years ago. It was all so different from the difficulties Adam McKendrick had tried to prepare me for.

"This place sure has prettied up since I was in here last," Father remarked as we stopped before the elevators. I started to agree about the new tower with its *Penthouse* for cocktails, the many changes. But I caught his grin and significant nod at the Japanese girl, exquisite in her kimono and obi, who was directing us to the first elevator. I had been a little late in noticing what Father meant by "prettied up." He was so right! And so typically my father!

"I hope these are the inside elevators," I murmured as the doors opened. "Those glass bugs crawling up the outside of the building scare me to death."

"Here we are!" Father broke off my excuses, waving me into the car. Although the interior was dark, the glass walls gave it away. I stopped abruptly, but others besides Father were piling in behind me. There was nothing to do but allow myself to be pushed forward, against the far glass window. The elevator began to move amid the giggles and chatter of thrill-seekers around me.

Father put a hand on my shoulder. "Easy, Honey!" He could tell how nervous I was, but I was also angry at myself for allowing an old experience to upset me. The giggling around us grew more intrusive. We had risen above the surrounding shaft and were rapidly passing beyond the back of the old, familiar half of the hotel.

"Look!" someone cried. "The B-of-A Building!

And there's the Mark up on the hill!" Others picked up the identifications. It became a game with them.

I forced myself to look out. At a distance the Oakland Hills looked soft and shimmering under the reflected glow of sunset. The great links of the Bay Bridge seemed alive with traffic. Those distant views did not turn my stomach or sicken me as did the sudden, jolting sight of the rooftops and Post Street below us. I swallowed once, then again, and concentrated on the frame of the window while my stomach seemed to drop. Then, as the elevator stopped, my stomach slowly righted itself.

Everyone poured out into the foyer of the *Penthouse* cocktail lounge. Breathing rapidly, and with my knees weak as water, I walked beside my father. He was still not aware of the severity of my fears. He talked about the excitement of the ride and the view, wondered what the hotel rooms in the Tower were like, and added wryly, "Not that I'm likely to find out. There's lots of places nearer my speed."

"What are you doing these days?" I asked, trying to get my mind off the absurd and yet haunting terror of the return ride down that outside elevator. There must be an inside, closed elevator somewhere.

Father and I were led to a corner overlooking Post Street, all too far below.

"What'll you have, Hon? How about a nice whiskey sour? You don't want to get used to the hard stuff, not at your age."

I didn't remind him of my present age, but I did oblige him by ordering a bloody mary. Father ordered rye and water.

"Now then, Sprout, you asked me what I'm doing these days. I expect your investigators told you all about it, but . . ."

"No," I said honestly. "He hasn't—they haven't said a word. Just that you were employed."

The drinks came. Father watched me a little anxiously as I stirred my drink with its celery-stalk "stirrer." I drank slowly as he began on his rye.

"I guess you'll do, Hon. Don't want any alkies in the family. My Dad died stinking drunk. Don't want it to get to be a tradition, or anything." I laughed and he went on with one of those heavy shrugs I remembered, as if his clothes didn't quite fit his big shoulders. "To get on to the matter at hand, I run a little museum thing down beyond the Cannery. Along Fisherman's Wharf. Miniature sailing vessels, mini-wrecks. And then, some big exhibits behind them."

"Like the Maritime Museum?"

"Well . . . like a kind of maritime horrors show. For four bits you get into a cabin on the Titanic, or the Doria. Or the Morro Castle. Or the Lusitania . . . that's a rough one. Torpedoes, you know. She sank in eighteen minutes. Of course, it's all in fun. A lot of shrieking and laughs. The kids love it."

"Sounds morbid to me," I muttered, drinking hastily. His talk of Titanic and Doria staterooms made me think of claustrophobia and my fear of the elevator I would probably have to take down to reach the street again. In my nervousness I began to chew up the celery stirrer, an act that my father found amusing.

"Funny little kid. You still stewing about that damn . . . darned elevator? Can't bite you, you know."

"It did once," I said flatly.

"Sure," he agreed, "but how often do those accidents happen? Anyway, you're safe here. Just keep thinking that."

I nodded, but my smile wobbled a little. Inside, I was seething with a sudden, horrifying doubt.

Because, of course, my accident in a hotel elevator—a fall of three floors under slowly gathering momentum—had occurred in Madrid, Spain, six years ago. One of the elevator's occupants, a Venezuelan tourist, had suffered a broken leg. The other three of us, two Spanish ladies and I, were badly bruised and shaken. But aside from an item in a local paper, the matter had been quickly hushed up. Yet here was my father, in San Francisco, accepting my fear of elevators and my mention of the accident without question or even curiosity!

I said almost too casually, "Do you get away from California very often?" It seemed the only possibility, that he had been in Europe at that time and somehow heard about the accident.

"Nope. Got my operation on the Wharf to look after. Doing pretty well, if I do say so. Not—" he added, "—that it couldn't do better. You can always do better."

He is going to ask me for money, I thought. I had intended eventually to share with him, make his life easier, if he turned out to be the real Tom Tracey, but once my suspicions had been aroused, I found it hard to quiet them.

"I suppose other people invest in your exhibit," I said, giving him an opening.

He boomed out a quick, surprising denial. "No. And I don't want 'em, neither. Partners clutter up a business. I built the whole damn thing myself. Not the springs underneath, of course, but the boxes—they're the staterooms, and the sound effects and whatnot. Nope. I'm talking about business. It's slowed a little in this recession we've got going. My—well, my cashier, Leah Chandragar, she's pretty sharp about the moola. And she beefs a lot."

I guessed that Leah Chandragar, Father's cashier, was probably his girlfriend. It was not surprising. He was a very virile, masculine man, but his remark did make me very curious about the cashier who was "pretty sharp about the moola." I hoped I would like her. I had pictured being friends with any new family that he might have acquired in the long years of our separation.

"I'd love to see your exhibit," I said quickly. "Maybe we could have dinner together soon . . . whenever you are available."

"Me? Available? Honey, an old man like me, he's available any evening you're free. Leah said I was to—" Obviously, he decided to amend this. "Anyway, I'm free. Sometimes Leah and I, we grab a bite at one of the Wharf joints together, not the big, fancy tourist places, but—well, when there's any crab in, it's mighty good. And the chowder's best in the world. Maybe you'd—ah—how about you meeting Leah some time? Just to say how-do. She's a mighty interesting female. Great-grandfather was a rajah, so she says."

"I'd love to meet her." But I played nervously with what remained of my celery stick, trying to take up time. I had no objection to meeting Father's friend, the rajah's great-granddaughter. In fact, I was very curious to meet her. But I wanted to put off the downward flight in that glass elevator as long as possible.

Father was looking over my head at the people entering the *Penthouse* from the elevator and though I was busy with my drink, I was sure he gave a startled little jolt suddenly, as if he had seen someone he recognized. I looked up just in time to catch the gesture. I decided to pretend I hadn't noticed.

"Nothing left in that drink but ice, Barby," he warned me, adding with a jovial ease that did not quite conceal his haste, "Shall we amble on down to the Wharf? Have some cracked crab, or whatever?"

I was not surprised. As I got up, I felt that his haste fitted in with the curious little start which betrayed him a minute before. There was a great crowd in the center of the room, waiting for our table and others commanding the best view. He had chosen a time to leave which would let us lose ourselves in that crowd as we hurried out to the elevators. The crowd closed in behind us after we left.

Mischievously, as we stepped into the waiting elevator, I said to Father, "Someone is running for this car. Shall we wait? But already, he had reached around me and pressed the first floor button. The doors closed. I wondered whom he was trying to avoid. But a second later, when I gripped my hands together in stiff-fingered terror, as the elevator descended, he was his own easy, fearless self, chattering on about the skyline, trying to take my mind off what obviously scared me, and wondering aloud whether it would be easier to get a taxi than the cable car this time of night, when the taxi rush was at its height.

CHAPTER 2

I was so busy praying I'd reach terra firma without a major disaster, either to the elevator or my nerves, that I did not think again about Father's unwanted acquaintance in the *Penthouse* until we were walking through the main-floor lobby again. He was being careful now, not looking around too intently, but I could have sworn he was on the watch, all the same.

"Who was your friend up there?" I asked very casually.

"Fella always borrowing money. Since the show's making it, I get a lot of old friends showing up. Sometimes in pretty odd places."

He spoke quickly, easily—too quickly and too

easily to be quite on the level with his answer. It was as if he had spent the time in the elevator figuring out an answer to a question that might or might not come. But this was all very much like Father. I had loved him as a child and enjoyed his company, but I didn't need Mother's warnings to inform me that you couldn't believe everything Tom Tracey told you.

"And they follow you clear up the Tower?" Then I laughed, playing it lightly. "You always were an awfully popular man. I remember that time when you and Mother and I had finished Sunday brunch at the Cliff House and that longshoreman followed us clear into Sutro Baths, claiming you owed him twenty dollars." I was silent then, my heart thumping, as I waited for him to fall into my trap.

Father frowned, slapped his forehead like a comic and said, "Barbara-Jane Tracey, you either have me mixed up with some other Dad or you've caught me with a bad case of amnesia."

"What do you mean?"

"I've been a lot of places where I shouldn't be in my day, but whether or not I should have been in Sutro Baths, I never was. Matter of fact, seems to me the old place is gone now."

"A couple of years ago, they say."

He glanced at me quizzically. "Testing the old man, Sprout?"

I felt my cheeks redden in what must have been

a dead giveaway. I reached out and put my arm in his. "Hi, Dad!"

We crossed the entire lobby to Powell Street in complete harmony. On my part, at any rate. We had started down the steps when a man's voice called to us from the sidewalk.

"Hello there, Miss Tracey . . . Mr. Tracey. Small world!"

"Who the devil is that?" my father wanted to know, and then recognized the tall figure of Adam McKendrick striding toward us with that innocent smile which always annoyed me by what I considered its superiority.

"You!" I greeted him with an all too obvious lack of enthusiasm. "You can stop spying on him now. He really is my father."

But Father was more forgiving. "Here, here, girl. He was only doing what you hired him to do. "Evening, McKendrick. I guess you heard. I've been checked out okay. Even my girl says so."

Nothing upset my private eye.

"Great! Maybe you'll let me buy you two a drink. To your new family, Tracey. That is to say —your old family."

I wondered if Father understood the sardonic doubt in that friendly suggestion. *New family*, indeed!

"No, thank you," I said. "You are too late. We've had our drink. Now we're going down to the Wharf for dinner. And to see Father's exhibit.

I think you must have forgotten to tell me how well he is doing in his business."

Adam McKendrick kept coming on, like somebody who is repeatedly being shot and doesn't know it.

"Did I forget? I wonder how I came to do that. Well, let me make up for it by taking you both to dinner. I haven't seen this exhibit of yours, Tracey. Sounds promising. I was always a sucker for a good show."

I started to object, supposing this was just his way of being sarcastic, but to my surprise, Father said in the friendliest way, as if he meant it,

"Good! You'll get a kick out of it. Lot of thrills there. But one thing we're all agreed on, Mac. I'm taking you and my daughter to dinner. You've spent enough on me, you and your private eye crowd."

"Sorry about that." Adam was all friendly sincerity, but he still seemed, to me at least, on guard beneath that pleasant smile.

My father went on. "Don't think I'm complaining. You've done me a big favor, bringing us together. Okay now. I really mean it. You're both my guests. Look! While you get a taxi and hold it, I'll cash a check in the hotel. Meet you at the cab."

He had loped away from us back into the hotel before Adam and I quite realized what he was doing.

"It's all very well that he isn't after my money,"

I complained, "but this is ridiculous. You invited yourself along. Why should poor Father have to cash checks and invite us? It should be the other way around."

But Adam had already taken my hand and I found myself practically galloping down the steps, to the sidewalk where the doorman hailed a taxi. More or less under the influence of all this man-handling, I found myself scrambling over the back seat of the cab and expecting Adam and Father to join me. Instead, my private eye left me there and dashed back under the canopy and up the steps. I watched through the open cab door until he came tearing back.

"Spying again?" I demanded coolly.

Adam McKendrick leaned in the open door.

"He's not cashing a check, if that's what you mean."

I knew it! I thought. This fellow was born a negative thinker.

"And what is he doing?"

"Signing something."

"Of course. A check."

"Not a check. Looked to me like a page from a hotel note pad."

I sighed elaborately. "A note for the Mafia. Or at the very least, his fellow conspirators." I thought he would laugh. It was disconcerting to have that straight, blue-eyed gaze fixed upon me in a thoughtful way.

"A note to someone, anyway."

"Get in!" I commanded. "Or get out. Don't straddle the cab."

This time he did laugh and got in, suggesting I move over to the middle of the seat. "Far be it for me to come between Father and daughter."

We changed seats, scraping by each other with difficulty, so that it was almost impossible not to squeeze ourselves into a good humor. By the time Tom Tracey came out of the hotel, Adam and I were both laughing at his effort to fold his legs up until they accommodated the small size of the cab.

"That's what I like to see. You two kids made up?" Father asked when he joined us.

"We never quarrel. Your beautiful daughter simply doesn't approve of private investigators. I hope you don't share that prejudice, Tom."

Father insisted such an idea was absurd. "And to prove it, I just left a message at the desk, letting my daughter's boyfriends know she's out on the town with a private eye."

Adam and I exchanged glances. "Aha!" I taunted him.

Father looked at each of us, puzzled. We made no effort to explain and Father signaled to the equally puzzled taxi driver.

"We're off now. Sorry to've kept everyone waiting."

"No problem," the driver announced, pulling out and skimming the tires over the humming cable that bisected the street. "Meter's been running. Where to?"

"Hyde Street Pier," Father called. "Or make it Beach Street at the foot of the hill. We can walk the last block."

After a little burst of inane discussion over what hill in San Francisco was the most breathtaking, there was an uncomfortable little silence. Every subject that Adam McKendrick brought up sounded, to my hypersensitive ears, like a test being applied to Tom Tracey.

"Tell me how you two met," I said finally, almost too abruptly, and then made matters worse by hurriedly adding, "I don't want to pry. I mean—all that investigating business was pretty silly. But—what did you think, Father, when you saw that ad in the paper? Do you always read the *Personals?*"

Adam was about to speak but said nothing. Instead, he leaned forward a little to watch Father's reaction to my question. In spite of my belated fears, Father was undisturbed, almost eager to reminisce over the moment he discovered his lost daughter was looking for him.

"Well, Honey, I don't pay any mind to those ad-things usually. And to tell the truth, I didn't see the ad you put in. You know, that stuff's for the womenfolk, mostly."

"But then, how—?" What troubled me most, I think, was that I felt the stiffening and tension in

Adam McKendrick's body close beside me. Why did he find everything about my father so intriguing? It was Adam who had told me that this Thomas Michael Tracey passed all the "tests," including fingerprints.

"How? We've got Leah to thank for bringing us together. Good old Leah! She's a dear old girl. But you have to know her well to—ah—appreciate her. Not like your mother, Sprout. Not at all like your mother."

I didn't quite know how to take this. I could think of many ways in which Mother had failed as a wife. Even at the age of five I had heard her sharp, elegant voice at night, warning Father that he was "an animal," that she was bored with his "uncouth" desires, and that "if he fancied she was going to produce an entire litter of Irish brats he was badly mistaken." I rightly concluded that Mother regarded me as the first in this line of unwanted "Irish brats."

"Not like Mother," I repeated slowly. "No. But then, not many are as beautiful as she was. Everyone always said that."

Father's voice lost a trifle of its Irish lilt. He sounded almost expressionless.

"All of that. I know I thought so. You—pretty as you are—you're not a patch on your mother. But I've a notion a nice, warm Irish lass with a pretty smile has a whole lot more to offer than a flawless beauty like—well, you know who. Wouldn't you say that, Adam?"

I waited a trifle apprehensively for Adam McKendrick's verdict, which was absurd because from the very first his self-assurance had rubbed me the wrong way. It didn't help matters when he waited a few seconds before he gave a highly qualified agreement, adorned by that mischievous smile of his.

"I would certainly say it—if the young lady ever flashed any of her charm upon me. Unfortunately—"

I tried to look indifferent but failed. I wanted very much to say, "Who cares?" but I wasn't that good an actress. I did want to be thought attractive by any young man, even my supercilious friend.

"So your friend Miss Chandragar saw my ad," I went on, to Father, ignoring Adam. "Then you called Mr. McKendrick's office?"

"The lady called my office," Adam put in. "I believe Tom here had to be persuaded. Or do I have it wrong?"

The driver called out, "Here we are, folks." He pulled up at the foot of the Hyde Street hill. Before us, another block or two beyond the little Aquatic Park, was the Golden Gate, still dotted with sailboats like pale moths against the choppy water of evening. On the near horizon the Golden

Gate Bridge lights had just flashed on. Father started to point out the changes since my childhood, and Adam paid the driver.

"That's the Cannery on our right, that clutch of old brick buildings. Couple of great little restaurants there. And shops. Ever been in the place?"

"No, Father. Is Adam right? Did you have to be persuaded to contact his office?"

"Sort of. Listen, Honey, did you ever eat crepe asparagus? They've got a great little place up on the second floor of one of those old Cannery buildings. You can get about a hundred different crepes, if that's your thing. Leah and I go there a lot. I thought we'd pick up Leah and maybe chew up a little something."

Adam had joined us by this time. I was still confused by the crepe asparagus and I could see that he had heard this too. For the first time I didn't resent his amusement. He was careful to confine his smile to his eyes, however. Their expression was surprisingly friendly as he agreed with Father while explaining what it was all about.

"Provincial French crepes. Very good, too. Place called *La Manche*. What do you say?"

I suspected both Adam and Father were trying to pave the way for the meeting between Father's lady friend and me by surrounding the meeting with good food and a restaurant that might be a conversation piece. I appreciated their efforts, but I couldn't quite figure out why the idea of meeting

Father's lady should shake me up so they had to "pave the way."

"Great!" I said, taking Father's arm. "How far is your exhibit from here? And on our way, you can tell me what you thought . . . how you felt when Miss . . . your friend told you she'd talked to Adam's office."

On my other side Adam McKendrick took my arm and we strolled briskly down the street to the Wharf, past the small stands, smelling of fresh-cooked seafoods, past a ship-chandler's shop, souvenir stores, the mini-harbor crowded with boats of the crab fleet, though I'd heard there wasn't much crab these days. There were several fancy restaurants. But before that, on the city side of the street, was a huge, barn-like brick structure about two and a half stories high. The windows were seated with boards. The whole place wouldn't have looked like much more than a heap of ancient bricks ready to topple at the first earth tremor, except for the big, gaudy painted sign above the open front door:

YOU ARE THERE
SEA DISASTERS
THOS. M. TRACEY, Captain.

I was amused at the title Father had chosen. Apparently, he had no objection to identifying himself with some remarkably unlucky skippers.

Just outside the door was the box office, a wooden box topped by glass through which we could see a dark woman tearing off tickets from a large roll. Two long-haired customers of indeterminate sex glanced at the tiny ticket-ends they received, then went through the turnstyle that barricaded the doorway, without glancing at the collection of blown up pictures which revealed all the horrors of major sea disasters.

"Your exhibit is doing business," I told Father, happy for him.

He shrugged. "That's only two bits to get in. Then they choose whatever 'staterooms' they want. Four bits each." No one since Mother and I left San Francisco twenty years ago had ever referred to a half-dollar as *four bits*. "You want fire at sea, you've got the Morro Castle. Maybe it's a hot day. You pick the Titanic. Icebergs, you know."

I shuddered, and Adam summed up my own feeling by remarking, "In other words, your customers don't have to be masochists, but it helps."

We all laughed.

We crossed the street together, Father waving to the woman in the makeshift box office. I could make out her dark hair and imagined her eyes were dark, piercing, as she looked out at us. She did not return Father's wave. I don't know about Adam, but I was intimidated by that level, unsmiling stare. Was Leah Chandragar, for some obscure reason, an enemy?

Almost immediately I was thrown for a loss by the woman's extraordinary change of mood. We walked toward her, and suddenly she flashed a toothy smile. She was a good-looking woman with vaguely exotic features. Her eyes had an oblique slant, her cheekbones were flat and prominent, and her even, unblemished flesh was almost saffron colored. She looked to be in her early forties, or at any rate in her late thirties. But her flashing white teeth, which all looked real and very serviceable, made me think suddenly of Red Riding Hood's wolf.

She got off her perch gracefully, patting the thick, old-fashioned bundle of black hair at the nape of her neck. Opening the door at the back of the booth, she came around to greet us. She looked strikingly tall and elegant in a black Chinese *Chongsam*, its straight line adding to her imperious look. Poor Father! He always did get involved with imperious women.

Leah Chandrager was an irresistible force, however. She came to us with beautiful, long hands outstretched, and almost before we could speak, she had taken my wrists and drawn me to her.

"My dear little girl! Forgive me . . . do I shock you with my familiarity? But I seem to have known you for a lifetime. Through your dear father. Tom, you told me she was pretty, but even you did not do her justice. And those pictures you showed me! Childlike. Charming. But not this lovely young lady."

I was overwhelmed by all this praise, and by the imposing beauty of the woman herself. I found myself thinking, like an impressed child: *This fascinating woman likes me . . . she was the one who brought me and my father together . . .*

I smiled my gratitude, mumbled something I don't remember, and was relieved when she moved on to shake hands with Adam McKendrick. She appeared to know him better than I had expected. I studied his reaction. He seemed to be more than a little interested in her, which was not surprising, although, cattily, I decided she was about ten years older than Adam.

"Mrs. Chandragar—Leah! Good to see you again." So she was *Mrs.* Chandragar. "We owe you a great deal, all of us. I still remember that first call of yours, to the office."

Father was grinning at them and silently drew me closer to watch this little byplay.

Leah agreed quickly, enthusiastically, with Adam.

"And well do I . . . I shall call you Adam. I was quite frightened that day, I may tell you. It was not my affair, and yet, I could not let poor Tom's pride stand between him and the little daughter he loved so much. I called your office, received . . . what is it called?"

"The runaround, I believe," Adam volunteered good-naturedly. "But your persistence paid off."

"Paid off!" Leah wrinkled her elegant nose. "What an unfortunate choice of words!"

"Nevertheless, you convinced Tom to surrender. And enriched the lives of all concerned."

Enriched? I glanced at Adam. He seemed to be full of unfortunate, double-meaning phrases, but he was flashing the friendly, innocent look and I did not know what to think as he and Mrs. Chandragar exchanged compliments.

A terrible racket inside the museum interrupted all this chit-chat. Startled, I swung around and stared into the darkness beyond the turnstyle. The noise was punctuated by hideous sounds of human beings in pain. Even Adam stopped exchanging edged compliments.

"What's that? The Mutiny on the Bounty?"

"Nope," Father said proudly. "Lusitania's been hit amidships by a torpedo. That's the screams of the dead and dying. Sound track we worked out. There's another torpedo coming."

"How horrible!"

They all looked at me. For the first time in our acquaintance, I had a feeling that Adam and I were on the same wavelength. Neither Father nor Mrs. Chandragar understood me. Of that I was sure. The lady stared. Father patted me on the shoulder.

"Hon, it's all make-believe. You want your old man on relief, or something? Took me eight years to figure this one out. You got to give folks a few thrills. Especially the kids. They demand realism. So we worked out a sound track: screams . . . panic . . . whistles . . . steam escaping . . . the works. Well, you heard it."

"I certainly did."

"It's make-believe, Sprout, like the stories I used to tell you when you were ankle high. But it sure pays off. Especially with the teeners. And the hippies. They've got lots of pocket cash. The hippies."

I looked back into the darkness. Through the screams and the roaring and the hideous sound effects created by my father, I began to make out the giggles and laughter of the pair who had gone inside, and of other visitors. There were more sounds effects, punctuated by the amusement and pleasant terror of other customers.

"Let's go," I said. "I'm hungry." It was the first thing I could think of.

Father said, a little hurt, "Don't you want to see the exhibit? It's interesting. Took a lot of imagination and elbow grease and research. That was Leah's department. We worked like dogs. Didn't we, Leah?"

I was relieved to see that Leah understood me better than Father. "Tom, tomorrow is better. Or another day. Shall we go to dinner now? Chato can take care of the exhibit while we are gone. He is working on the broken heating unit of the *Morro Castle*. I will call him; shall I?"

"It might be best," put in Adam. He glanced at me. I thought his glance was friendly, warm.

With a reluctance we all noted, Father agreed. "Too bad. I'm not ashamed of the exhibit. Not at all. But I guess we can go into that some other time. You say Chato's inside?"

He left us abruptly, pushed through the turnstyle after pressing a button on the inside wall beyond the turnstyle. We all looked after him. I wasn't sure whether I echoed Adam's thoughts when I studied the way Father had vanished and said, "What happens when they exit into that darkness? Do they all dissolve in a puff of smoke? I'm not sure it's very safe to try out Dad's disaster game."

As if in answer we all heard a series of grating but happy giggles, and three girls in mini-skirts came out of what apparently was a side passage and pushed past us, through the turnstyle.

"Marvy!" one of them cried.

"Groovy! I never thought I'd feel . . . I tell you, it was hairy! We've got to take the monsters next time."

"Right on! Next time make it the Titanic, or whatever. Jody's monster would eat that. That *Morro Castle* was too damned hot."

They went trailing off down the street, leaving Mrs. Chandragar and Adam and me in a state of high amusement. I think I summed up their conclusion when I admitted, "That's one threesome who weren't scared. Does everyone react like that?"

Mrs. Chandragar assured me, "Everyone. You see, it is an amusing thrill. That was our intention. To combine the experiences with history. . . . Ah, here is Tom. Have you told Chato we will be going to dinner?"

"All set. Chato's taking over. He said Verne will be in before eight. He can handle the box office."

Mrs. Chandragar nodded, smiling her toothy smile.

"Good. I knew you wouldn't enjoy dinner if Chato had his hands in the till."

"Not much! But Verne won't let him get away with anything. Shall we go, folks?"

Mrs. Chandragar took my arm. "We shall walk together and become very acquainted. You cannot imagine how long I have looked forward to this meeting."

"Thank you. We owe you a great deal for bringing us together."

"Dear child!" she murmured in her fulsome way.

I looked back at the big, gaudy museum. A wizened little man of about forty or so came out and climbed into the box office. He appeared to have broken his back at some time and my first instinct was sympathetic. But he looked up at that minute. I was shocked by the malevolence in that glance.

"Is that Verne?" I asked curiously.

Leah Chandragar glanced around. "Heavens, no! That's Chato. He and Tom used to work the docks together. Verne is quite a different affair. My son. He is like a son to Tom. But I shouldn't be talking like this to Tom's legitimate daughter. I'm sure Tom would prefer to tell you about Verne himself. Let's not think any more about it. Poor Verne! During the riots last year on the waterfront they actually accused him of murder. Nothing could be more absurd. He is a delightful boy. Let's not think any more about it."

Easier said than done!

CHAPTER 3

We all sat eating the delicious crepes, which had looked to me like big manila envelopes when they were served. But when I cut into mine with my fork, the tender, delicately seasoned chicken and asparagus seeped out and, in other circumstances, would have melted on my tongue.

My thoughts got in my way. I said I would like it if I found I had a brother. Now, I was worried that this Verne would be forced on me as a brother. Was it because he may have killed someone? Or merely that I don't want a stranger as a close relation?

I couldn't answer my own question. If I hadn't seen and heard Leah Chandragar's effusive friendliness, I could almost suspect her of maliciously enjoying my uncertainty during dinner.

I was still trying to get more information about the unsavory Verne when Leah and Adam resumed their discussion about the discovery of my connection with my father.

Adam was saying, "How did you persuade Tom to submit to all our—I believe he called it persecution, when we investigated him?"

Mrs. Chandragar put a hand out, rested it briefly on my father's freckled, callused hand.

"Occasionally he listens to me. I reminded him of how he had adored his little daughter's memory for so many years."

But he never looked me up, or corresponded with me during the twenty years of our separation. I had been a poor daughter, maybe, but did Father really care about me all those years? I wished I could have some proof.

"Did you really keep track of me all those years, Father?"

"Sure did."

"But why didn't you write to me? No matter what Mother did, I would have found a way to answer you."

Adam looked amused, I thought, as he pursued my question. "Yes. Why didn't you, Tom?"

I caught the slight, ever so slight glance exchanged between Father and Mrs. Chandragar. The woman's dark eyebrows arched.

"One could hardly expect a man of Tom's pride to go where he was so clearly unwanted. I'm afraid, my dear Barbara, one must—reluctantly—place the responsibility with your mother. A very cold woman. No sentiment there."

Curiously enough, although I privately agreed with her opinion of Mother, I very much resented this woman's statement. After all, she hadn't actually known Mother, nor could she possibly know all the details of Mother's divorce from Father. Certainly she wouldn't know Mother's side. If there was one.

"Then you did follow my life the whole time? I suppose you knew when I went abroad. Or away to school."

"Sure did," said Father proudly, with his mouth full and waving his fork. "More or less."

"It is strange that your mother never married again, my dear," put in Leah. "One might have thought a woman with her . . . background would have found another husband almost at once."

"But Mother liked to have her own way. I suppose she may have frightened some of her boyfriends. She certainly had plenty." Almost before the woman spoke, I knew I had led her into an indiscretion.

"Still, such a matter is very small compared to the inducement of the lady's fortune. I mean . . ."

"Precisely. A fortune makes up for a good

many less admirable qualities." Adam's quick covering up of her blunder annoyed me so much I wanted to kick him in the shins under the table.

"And now I'm in the same spot," I said brightly, bringing the subject right back. I wanted to see if Mrs. Chandragar would give away a significant interest in my inheritance. But to my speechless amazement, it was my ankle that was kicked under the table. Furious, I looked up just in time to catch a slight raising of Adam's eyelids. Definitely a warning. I closed my mouth, but I didn't like it.

Father assured me, "Yes, but you don't need a fortune. My kid doesn't need anything but just her own nice, warm personality: isn't that a fact, Adam?"

"Certainly is. Just as well, too. Her legal-eagles tell me she's all wrapped up in trusts. No one to get a hand on it. I only hope my firm gets paid. How about that, Barbara?"

I said, "I'll do my best to see they pay you . . . What a darling place this is! All those copper kettles on the wall back there. And the costume of the waitress. Have you noticed? Exactly like rural France." I glanced at my wristwatch. "You know, I hadn't expected to be out so late. And I really am expecting a rather important phone call at the hotel tonight."

Mrs. Chandragar waved a coy finger.

"Ah-ha! That sounds like a romance. Tom, are

you sure you approve? This girl of yours shouldn't be wasted on just any young man. She might be the victim of some fortune hunter."

"You forget," I said sweetly, "I am twenty-five. Much too old to need parental permission. And he's such a doll! Too bad he has no money, but the cute ones never have." I sighed. I could see that Adam McKendrick was getting more annoyed by leaps and bounds. Could he guess that the whole thing was a put-on, that there was no late-evening call expected? "And he is so awfully irresistible," I went on.

Everyone began to get ready to leave, but I felt uncomfortably sure that my lie about the phone call had done more than annoy Adam. It had caused Leah Chandragar to tense up and even Father was alert, either worried or anxious, or both.

"I'll take Barbara home," Adam volunteered. "You have your box office to get back to. No need in your making the trip into town."

There was a short dispute between Leah and Father. She agreed with Adam McKendrick that he should take me back to the hotel and something in her decisive tone made me suspect she wanted a little serious conversation with Father. Did she want to prime him on his conduct with me?

We all walked down to the Beach Street level together. Father kissed me and Mrs. Chandragar murmured warmly. "I feel that Tom's dear ones are my dear ones. Forgive me, Barbara." She put her hands on my shoulders and pressed a very dry kiss upon my cheek. "Let me be a mother to this motherless little girl of yours, Tom." Embarrassed, I patted one of her hands and tried not to release myself too quickly.

Adam and I watched the two of them walk rapidly down the street, Mrs. Chandragar keeping pace with my father, thanks to the side split in her Chinese sheath. When they had gone about half a block, she began to talk to Father, waving her hands and being very vehement about what clearly was advice.

"Out of the frying pan, into the fire," I remarked, more or less to myself as Adam and I started for Aquatic Park and the turntable where a cable car was being pushed and pulled around toward the steep Hyde Street hill.

"What frying pan, and which fire?" he wanted to know.

"From Mother to that woman."

He laughed. Then, motioning toward the turntable, he asked, "Cab? Or car?"

"Car. It passes the St. Francis anyway; doesn't it? I'll beat you there."

We began to run. I don't know why I should have been impressed by Adam McKendrick's singular lack of gallantry in not only racing me, but winning; yet I was. He leaped onto the car and held out his hand to me, helping me to jump up beside him onto the moving cable car. As usual, there was a crowd, but we squeezed onto the outside seat and huddled close in the windy San Francisco evening as the car rattled over Beach Street and started up to the first level of the hill at North Point.

"Now, what do you think of dear old Dad?" Adam asked me as the car tilted up and we grabbed for anything handy to keep from sliding back into a slim hippy beside me.

"Father is—fascinating."

Adam agreed. "All of that."

"It's only . . . I do wonder a little about Mrs. Chandragar."

"I'm not surprised."

He fell into me. I fell against the bony shoulder of the hippy on my other side, and we laughed. At least, Adam and I laughed. The young man next to me, a little pressed by the weight of several human beings piled against him, winced and looked frightened. Adam leaned over my body to inform him: "You can get even with us later when we swing around on Nob Hill. Then, you can just fall against us."

"Yes, Sir," said the young man. He looked as if he thought we were in the last stages of a dangerous form of paranoia, and shrank into his thin denim jacket.

We began to climb, reached Bay Street two blocks up, and stopped long enough to pick up several more customers. It was dark by this time and the white fog of a late spring night was beginning to roll in.

I couldn't wait any longer. I stared at Adam until I got his attention away from the two girls in mini-skirts jumping on at that moment.

"I still haven't heard what you think about Mrs. Chandragar."

"What I think?" He laughed, not a very nice laugh, by which I assumed he wasn't too fond of Leah Chandragar. "Isn't it obvious? Your father's successor to the first Mrs. Tracey."

I bristled. "Don't be sarcastic. Mother was at least sincere about her likes and dislikes. And she had . . . class."

"That sounds a little snobbish. Don't you trust Mrs. Chandragar?"

"Really!" He was impossible. But it occurred to me as the cable car started up at what seemed a sharp forty-degree angle, that he might possibly be in the pay of Leah Chandragar. "She is charming," I added. "Beautiful, really."

"Hypocrite."

I didn't answer that. For one thing, the car was climbing at a breathtaking tilt, and for another, I was seriously beginning to mistrust him.

"If my accountants pay your company's bill, will you make enough to buy a car?"

"Good Lord!" He stared at me as the car climbed and we fell against each other again. "Why?"

"Well, you obviously travel by cab or other public transportation. Isn't that a little primitive for a man-about-town like you?"

"Not in this town. But as a matter of fact—I do own a car. I had no idea you were so snobbish you wouldn't travel in a public conveyance."

"That isn't so at all," I began, but was cut off by a sharp jolt, a push and pull, and then the car came to a complete stop. I was crushed between Adam McKendrick and the young hippy. Beyond Adam, a thin boy and girl were practically entwined, they were so close, but the pileup inside the car was more vocal. There were loud, nervous jokes punctuated by feminine squeals.

"What is it? Are we stuck?" I asked Adam. I didn't dare to move, I was so afraid the slightest shift would send us hurtling back down the hill to the bay.

"We're stuck. But don't worry. If the brakes had failed, we'd have gone minutes ago."

"My God!"

"Now, now . . . it's nothing to worry about." It was amazing how comforting his presence could be, this man I had disliked for weeks because of his flippancy, his nasty cynicism about my father.

"Let's get out of here!"

"Coward!" But he smiled. Behind him, I saw other people jumping off the car, a boy and girl, then a woman.

"Please . . . let's get off."

"Okay. But it's your idea." He leaped down, then turned to lift me off. The gripman up front was discussing a power failure with several pleasantly excited teen-agers. We left them to their thrills and, together, walked down two blocks to North Point. I was surprised at how dark it was between the street lights. I shivered.

Adam said, "It's all right now. Nothing to worry about. We'll walk over to Ghirardelli Square and call a cab."

"How far is that?"

He pointed to the old clock tower on the western horizon.

"Just a block or so."

At the same time a trolley-bus came hurtling around Van Ness Avenue in the distance and headed toward us. Several other refugees from the stalled cable car rushed out past us to hail the bus and I said suddenly, "Let's not wait. I want to get out of this car as soon as possible."

He looked at me, a little troubled, I thought, but he ushered me to the trolley-bus as it rolled to a stop. Once we were in our seats, I explained to Adam in a low tone, "I'm not usually quite such a coward. But there has been something tonight—some atmosphere that is scary. Don't you notice it?"

He smiled but without that appearance of superiority I had earlier imagined in his humor.

"I haven't noticed that exactly. But I do think we had better be a little cautious about those two."

I had no trouble guessing who "those two" were and felt my original, senseless resentment toward him because his organization had an investigator's natural suspicion.

"Not Father. It's the woman. I just don't trust her."

But his attention had shifted to the door of the bus which had squeezed shut. The bus was rolling away from the corner and I saw what had attracted his attention. A figure that seemed to be male had hurried up at the last minute only to miss the bus. He appeared dark-haired and was wearing a loose black slicker that glistened as it fluttered in the wind and fog.

"Do you know that fellow?"

Adam turned around, faced forward. His curious behavior had others looking back, but we were now turning into Columbus Avenue and the man who missed the bus was left far behind, out of sight. A fellow behind Adam tapped him on the shoulder in a friendly way.

"Don't worry, old man. There's always another bus."

"Sure thing, old man."

I nudged him. "Who was he? Anybody we know?"

Adam said after a few seconds, "I can't be sure.

I just thought, for a minute—well—it doesn't matter now."

"You really are maddening."

He smiled but I think he was still concentrating on the flying figure who missed the bus. I moved away from him, stared out the window at the scattered lights of the North Beach district. I still remembered the delicious meals I'd had here as a child when Father took me to visit Italian friends. Then we came home, after our heavenly time, and Mother accused us of having garlic on our breath. Down came the lovely house of cards.

How dark it was out there!

Who *was* the man in the rain slicker? And why did Adam McKendrick act so secretive about it? I gave him the benefit of the doubt, that he simply wanted to keep me from worrying. I studied him furtively. I really knew very little about this man. The trouble was, I did know an attractive man when I saw one, and Adam met all the qualifications. I wanted him to be trustworthy.

The trolley-bus rumbled up through Chinatown and into the Stockton Street tunnel. Adam began to get up.

"Are we nearly there?" I asked, not entirely satisfied. I hadn't learned very much from him tonight; yet it seemed that we had been together a very long time. So much had happened since I met Father at six o'clock.

"We'll get off at Union Square," he said. "Your

hotel faces the west side of the Square. It's only a block to walk."

I reminded him, "You needn't have taken all this time getting me home. I appreciate it. I can't tell you how much."

"I wish you would." He grinned as he took my hand and held onto me when the bus came to a jolting halt. We clambered noisily off. The sidewalks around the Square were surprisingly deserted for such an early hour. It was not yet ten o'clock. The elegant, feminine display windows of I. Magnum's on the far south side opposite the Square attracted me and almost made me forget the peculiar malaise that gripped me. I was profoundly grateful for Adam McKendrick's tall figure and for his presence as he took my arm and more or less propelled me along the dark street toward the great hotel, which was only one block away but past a long series of intermittently light and dark shops.

I tried to take this long block of shadows casually.

"Look at those men's shirts in that window! I love shirts with a little originality . . . that design down the—" He was looking back over his shoulder. I broke off. He wasn't listening to me at all. I resented this and yet I had sense enough to know —or suspect—that he was concerned for my own safety when he paid no attention to my ramblings.

Just as we reached Powell Street, at the corner

of the hotel, a cable car rattled down the hill to a stop almost in front of us.

"Good heavens!" I exclaimed, studying the passengers. "It's our cable car. We reached here at the same time."

"Nice timing." He, too, was looking over the passengers. I wondered suddenly if he was searching for the person in the black slicker.

Since the cable cars always have the right of way and another was passing in the opposite direction on its way up the hill, we got a very good look at the passengers in the first car.

"Nothing there," I said casually to let him know he needn't keep secrets about our danger from me. And just what dangers might there be in that mysterious fellow with the flying slicker?

We crossed the street and went in the side entrance of the hotel. As we descended to the main floor level, I said, "I'm perfectly safe now. No runaway cable cars or glass elevators. If you have some other engagement tonight—"

He stopped in the middle of the hall and tilted my chin up with the knuckle of his forefinger. "Don't be sarcastic. You aren't the type."

I found myself rather overheated, either by the unmistakably sexual appeal of his touch, or by my indignation that he could so misunderstand my motives.

"As a matter of fact, I was trying to be nice! I assumed a man of your type was sure to have females lined up for dates like flies around a honey pot."

He grimaced. "I suppose I can consider myself lucky you don't compare me with bees and pollen! My job was to look after your interests. I'm doing that, and it includes inspecting your bedroom, your bathroom, and any other refinements rich young ladies find necessary to their comfort on their travels."

"Sitting room and two closets," I admitted in a small voice. He made me feel like Marie Antoinette taking bread from the mouths of babies.

By the time the elevator—inside and carpeted in luxurious red and black—reached my floor, my companion seemed to have forgiven me for enjoying a little luxury. He took my key and unlocked my door, made a thorough inspection of the suite with its elegant if uncomfortable eighteenth-century furnishings, and asked me if he should wait until I receive my all-important (and imaginary) phone call from Chicago.

"Don't be funny!" I said before I thought.

He looked at me, with a half-smile, as if trying to read my mind, and succeeded in making me very nervous.

Unable to keep wondering any longer, I burst out, "Tell me the truth! What are you afraid of? Am I in danger? And if so, why? And from whom?"

"Did it ever occur to you, my innocent, that

four million dollars makes a tidy motive for murder, especially from people whose lives have been fairly shady, up to now?"

Just what did he mean by that slur on poor Father?

"For your information, he doesn't know he is my heir! Furthermore, three-quarters of my estate goes to charity."

"Poor devil! So he and his loving little group only inherit one million."

"I haven't even signed the will yet. I . . ." Then I broke off, wondering why I must account for my actions to a near stranger whose sole purpose seemed to be to set me against my own father. I went on with as much quiet dignity as I could muster, "None of this is really your business, but as soon as I choose, I am to sign the will here in San Francisco. It's being drawn up by my boss's Coast partners."

"Who are they?"

I exhaled very sharply, to indicate I was fast losing my patience. I think the real reason he annoyed me was because he managed to keep me in a constant state of worry.

"D. Cossart and Merritte."

To my intense relief, he nodded and added the reassurance, "They're honest, anyway. Well, just remember what I said. Hold off on the will-signing bit for a while."

"But your own company assured me Father is genuine."

"Very true, and so far as we know, he is genuine. I still say—don't sign anything."

"Not even your check?" I went through the foyer to the hall door and held it open.

Since I left him no choice, he followed my sweeping, Grand Dame gesture, then turned back to me from the hall. This time there was a genuine twinkle in those good-looking eyes of his.

"What? No good-night kiss?"

I started to laugh but managed to close the door in his face, all the same. He really was impossible. But charmingly so.

Ten minutes later, as I was running my bath and wishing my housekeeper, Carrie, was here for me to talk to about the day's excitement, the telephone rang. I had an odd sensation of living in a particularly haunting dream. I had announced that I was expecting a call and here it was!

I took the bedroom phone and asked in a gingerly voice, "Who is this?"

The unmistakable teasing voice of Adam McKendrick answered me.

"What a tone to take when you are expecting the love of your life to call!"

"For heaven's sake! Haven't you got a home?"

"Certainly. Thanks to clients who pay us on time."

"I'll pay you! I'll pay you!"

Then his teasing faded. He said in a surprisingly kind voice, "Thought you'd like to know. I stopped and picked up the note your father left. And it was just as he said. A note to anyone who called you."

"I told you he was an honest man."

He evaded that. "Okay, now. Have we got everything straight?"

"I don't know about you, but it's all straight as far as I am concerned. Once again, good night, Mr. McKendrick."

He laughed. "This time it really is good night," and he hung up.

I sat down on the bed, wondering what in his conversation had troubled me. I had gotten so busy flirting with him that I forgot something of importance. Something about the will he had told me not to sign.

Then I heard the water still running heavily in the bathtub and rushed in to turn it off. There was a good deal of gurgling but, at least, it hadn't overrun the tub.

So there was nothing to worry about.

CHAPTER 4

Surprisingly enough, I slept soundly that night after the many excitements of the day. My hot bath evidently served its purpose and let me sleep uninterruptedly until the long distance telephone call awakened me at eight-thirty the next morning.

My first thought as I roused from that deep slumber was that my fake story to Father and Adam had come true: somebody was calling to say he was the love of my life.

My hand was shaking as I reached for the telephone, and I didn't really know why.

"Hello?"

"Barbara? Is this Barbara Tracey?"

I took a deep, long breath. "Oh. Hi, Boss." I

swallowed then and fumbled for the electric clock on the night stand. The clock's workings were set in an imitation of an eighteenth-century Parisian clock found in Marie Antoinette's *petit trianon*. I lifted it in my free hand, tried to focus on it.

"I had no idea it was so late." Then I began to wonder about the reason for this call. "How can I help you, Mr. Rivercombe?"

Glenn Rivercombe, of Rivercombe, Dawlish and Mead, had been in love with Mother for most of my lifetime. That was his trouble. Mother knew he would do anything for her; so she needn't marry him. He was a good-looking man in his fifties who avoided any permanent attachment by claiming allegiance "unto death and beyond" to a lost lover. It helped him a great deal with other women who found his silver hair and his impressive bulk irresistible. Occasionally, when he was about to shake off some attractive female client, suitably widowed and pursing hotly, he exchanged a wink with me. His "deathless love," had served him once again. It didn't keep him from weekly or even monthly affairs with those same beautiful clients, but it did protect him from the consequences.

"Whose heart have you broken since I left?" I joked.

He gave that heavy chuckle which had saved us many a headache on days when business or some court hearing went sour. "I'm working on it. But things aren't the same since your mother went. By the way, we've got a pool going here about you."

"Let me in on it. The pool, that is. What do I do to win it?"

"How are things progressing between you and that Adonis who calls himself a private eye?"

"I don't know any Adonises at the moment. And the only private eye I know doesn't call himself one. You called him that when you sent me to him."

"That's evading the issue. Remember when Gloria Pleven Jabowsky moved to Frisco? We gave her your friend McKendrick's name. She wanted to get evidence against Jabowsky. And you know what your dear Mother always said."

I really was shaken by that. "Don't tell me Mother knew him too!"

"No, no, my dear. She was—er—speaking of me, jokingly, when she said, 'A man you can't trust with another woman can often be trusted in business.' "

I laughed. "You really are a dog! Anyway, I think the reverse of Mother's theory is true. And incidentally, he advised me not to sign my will yet."

To my surprise Mr. Rivercombe agreed. "And good advice, too."

I remembered my fear of glass elevators and

falling cable cars and strangers with raincoats flying out like wings. "But what would happen if I were to die in an accident, say—the brakes on a cable car didn't work, or something."

"My Lord! Any danger of that?" I didn't answer and he called to the young woman who was taking my place, learning the legal end of the corporation in case I should move back to San Francisco for good. He rattled a file folder, obviously looking through some onion-skin pages.

"Here we are. Well, you know what it says. Most of the estate, at least—I would say—two-thirds, goes to your Mother. And if she dies with you, or predeceases you, it goes to your mother's second cousins in Milwaukee, Wisconsin."

I lamented, "But I don't even know them. I've never met them in my life."

"I'm afraid that didn't weigh heavily with your mother. This will is seven years old. It was made by your mother, in your interests."

And since Mother's death I had been reminded on several occasions that my will should be updated. It was really my fault that things were in such a mess. But at the age of twenty-five, I couldn't seem to picture myself in need of a will. People died because they were old, or sick, or in an air accident. Not Barbara-Jane Tracey.

. . . Or they died because they were in a crashing car. A cable car? Or they were murdered . . .

I said, "I'll think about it. And I'll talk to the

San Francisco law firm. I suppose I can trust them. Where are they located?"

"O'Farrell and Market. The Phineus Building. And—Barbara . . . ?"

"Yes?"

"If there should be anything—I'm sure they're first rate. They always have been. But if they make any difficulties, or if you find anything about them you don't like, please let me know at once. At the office or at home."

"Even if it's midnight, and you are in the arms of a beautiful blonde divorcee?"

He chuckled. "Especially then. You may be rescuing me from an old bachelor's fate-worse-than-death. . . . Promise, now?"

"I promise."

"And Barbara. Let us know if anything develops between you and our Adonis-friend. Wilkens says he has twenty dollars on McKendrick to show."

"Tell Wilkens I match his twenty that McKendrick runs last in a field of one."

"How are things coming along with your father? Are you absolutely sure of his identity?"

"No question about it. I even tried to trap him a couple of times, but he never failed me."

"Well—take care. It wouldn't be the first time a swindle was pulled of these proportions."

"I'll watch. But I know Father is—Father. I have absolute confidence in him, anyway."

"Anyway?"

"Nothing. I'm sure there is no problem. Is that all?"

"All. Except that the office misses you."

We said our good-byes and I put the telephone back. I thought over my plans for the day. I was not used to having entire days unplanned. This may have been one of the reasons why I had taken a business course after graduating from the Eastern and very elegant women's college chosen by my mother. I could not imagine spending my days as Mother had spent hers. It made my life far less gloomy after Mother's death. Maybe, I told myself now, this ambition to stay busy was something I inherited from my democratic father.

True. He hadn't always been hardworking. Or rather, he worked hard intermittently, and not always in the most honest labor. In some respects, I understood Mother's impatience with him. Much as I loved him, I wanted to be proud of him as well. It wasn't as if he couldn't be charming and hardworking at the same time, like Adam McKendrick.

"McKendrick! If the gang back at Rivercombe heard me now, I'd lose my bet." And be just another idiot female falling for that Don Juan who had so attracted Glenn Rivercombe's friend, Mrs. Gloria Jabowsky?

I banished McKendrick from my thoughts while I showered and dressed. Back home Carrie would have sent Mother's maid in with breakfast, whether I wanted it that way or not. As for me, I never could even remember whether the maid was named Marta or Marda. I had inherited her along with Mother's estate and both, while admirable, were not absolutely essential to my well-being.

During the days I had been in San Francisco waiting for final word from Adam McKendrick, I had eaten in what was, to me, an endless and fascinating series of restaurants. Some were hamburger joints, some were pancake parlors, some were of the delicious Chinatown cuisine, but I enjoyed them all almost as much as the greatest restaurants that Mother had frequented. I was myself at last, Barbara-Jane Tracey, a young secretary, looking for her father. The money, the expensive and much-too-large apartment that overlooked half of Lake Michigan and Chicago, these were behind me, along with Mother's housekeeper, her maid, her cleaning women and chauffeur, and endless accoutrements of modest wealth.

"I am your daughter, Tom Tracey," I told my reflection in the triple mirror, and I smiled, trying to make that smile look more like the mischievous Irish grin of Thomas Michael Tracey. I was only partly successful.

I wore a yellow suit, belted in the current style; the color was cheerful, bright, encouraging to me. But as I stared at my features and tried to find a resemblance to Father, I seemed to fancy a shadow behind my head. Another head, with hair darker than my own deep-brown hair, a face with an exotic cast, the high, sophisticated neck of a *Chongsam* sheath.

I refused to think about that. Or about my little doubts that may have been planted by Adam McKendrick. Maybe McKendrick has reasons for frightening me. Maybe, somehow, there was a profit in it for him if he turned me from my father. It was getting so I couldn't trust anyone.

Disgusted with myself for these absurd doubts I left hurriedly, took the elevator down and went across to the hotel's new Dutch coffee shop. While enjoying orange juice and breakfast pastry, I looked around casually at my fellow diners. I wasn't really thinking of them. I was wondering what I should do first this morning in this magic city.

A young man came in and was ushered to a small table at the other end of the room. His dark hair had been tousled by the wind. He appeared to be of middle height or a trifle shorter, not quite stocky, but not precisely thin either. He had an ingratiating grin as he looked up at the waitress. He was wearing a beat-up leather jacket and although he neither carried nor wore a shiny black rain slicker, I had a sudden hunch that he was the man Adam and I had seen running and failing to catch our bus last night. Somehow, I had expected to find him much more frightening. If, of course, he was the same man whose presence had stirred Adam to that curious uneasiness last night.

He ordered coffee and Danish, and was busy buttering the small round pastry when I finished my own breakfast and passed him on leaving the room. He stopped eating in order to watch me. He had attractive eyes, deep brown. I couldn't resist a dig at his interest in me.

"Butter's dripping," I remarked as I passed.

He caught himself, shook his fingers, and began to mop up things with his napkin. He was so busy and—I think—upset that he didn't see which way I went. As a matter of fact, I didn't know myself until I got out on the street and looked up and down, wondering anew at the clear, wind-washed sky, so unlike the air on the East Coast, though it did remind me momentarily of a windy Chicago day. I studied the street signs, found I was only a block above O'Farrell Street, where Rivercombe's San Francisco law firm associates were situated.

Without having decided ahead of time, I started down to O'Farrell. It also occurred to me that having made no plans ahead of time, I could hardly be followed by the young dark-haired man, unless he was a mindreader. I walked rapidly at first. Everyone around me seemed to be doing the same thing, although it was interesting to note that those on the sidewalk with me, or passing me, were the most cosmopolitan and democratic assortment I had ever seen.

Two bearded hippies in tie-dye outfits, one also wearing a fringed poncho, passed a small dark woman of great dignity, wearing the draped Indian sari in shadows of purple and gold, and coming toward me were a stout man and stout woman, obviously tourists, she in a calamitous mini-skirt and he in an orange flowered aloha shirt and Bermuda shorts. I looked after them, furtively amused, and saw at the same time that my dubious young dark-haired pursuer was not following me. This time I seemed to have fooled him, outfoxed him.

I walked a couple of blocks, past shops with names for the most part familiar from my childhood. When I was within a few steps of wide, perennially torn up Market Street which bisects the city, I found the old Phineus Building, one of those post-Victorian gothics that looked as though it had survived the Fire, though, of course, it hadn't. Like so many buildings in San Francisco, it was built on two levels. I entered an ancient, unadorned lobby, walked down a few steps, saw the Market Street entrance off to one side. For one unnerving second I thought I saw the dark-haired young man entering. Thank heaven, it was all an optical illusion! A perfectly innocent stranger, so far as I was concerned! Relieved, I went up to the second floor.

Although it was still early, the law firm was buzzing along busily in its quiet way. There were several conferences going on in cubbyholes, and I was received with the same cool, superior reserve that our own receptionist in Chicago used with unknowns who presumed on her time. She did recognize my name. Glenn Rivercombe had obviously been at work.

"Certainly, Miss Tracey. Mr. Cossart is in Los Angeles today. If only we had expected you! A letter. A telephone call. No matter. Mr. Merritte has someone with him right now. But I'm sure he will be free any minute." She put her hand on the inter com box. "I'll notify him you are here."

"No. Please don't. I have plenty of time." It would give me time to decide what I wanted to do about the will. There were a couple of large leather chairs, but I chose the eighteenth-century wooden settle, against the shocked protests of the receptionist. I didn't want to sink into one of those big, over-masculine chairs and become too comfortable. I had to sign the will making Father my major heir, or I had to allow those heirs chosen by Mother to become my heirs, and they were less known to me, far less loved, than my father. Third, I could make out a will to charities, a tentative will. But why? What had Father done to me that I should cheat him like this?

One more point emerged. I wasn't ill. I wasn't under a doctor's care. I was young, with my whole life before me. What was the rush? I was getting positively morbid on the subject. Or rather, I was being hounded on the subject by almost everyone who knew me. At least, they all considered it their business. It was maddening, because it kept planting the idea of my own death in my mind.

Luther Merritte came out of his office a few minutes later, passed me without a glance, shook hands with a portly gentleman and said good bye. I felt exceedingly self-conscious when the receptionist whispered something to him and he turned around, suddenly discovering me. The change in his manner was so abrupt I wanted to laugh. Mr. Merritte was a stoutish, balding man, carefully dressed with that rock-ribbed reserve which surprised me in a Californian. But then, as Father had once explained in my presence, "California is not San Francisco. And vice versa."

I hadn't understood it then. I scarcely understood it now. But there was no misunderstanding Luther Merritte's interest in the corporation of Rivercombe, Dawlish, Mead and their clients!

"Dear Miss Tracey! How do you do? We've been expecting you more or less daily the last two weeks. It is a pleasure to meet you at last. Glenn Rivercombe is an old friend of mine. He called me only two or three days ago on another matter but your name came up. Also the question of your legal residence in Illinois or in California. I believe you own property in both states. At any rate, we were wondering when you might drop in. Wills are very small matters when we are young and in the best of health. But . . ."

"I understand. I have been thinking about it very seriously. Especially since I met my father again after such a long time."

"Come into my office where we can be more comfortable. So you've actually met your father. I understand there was quite an investigation involved. Very romantic, as I told Glenn. Really a romantic business, finding one's father after practically a generation of . . ."

"Twenty years, really. And I was almost an infant at the time my parents were divorced."

"Yes, yes. So I was given to understand. And the incredible thing is that you managed to identify the fellow—sorry—your father, from your infantile memories of him."

I had to backtrack. "Not entirely infantile. I mean, I was five years old." You couldn't have many secrets with this outfit. "And I recognized him immediately."

His office was bright, airy and comfortably furnished, overlooking Market Street where something dusty and noisy was taking place, rather like the work of a monstrous mole. There was no air-conditioning, the theory having been explained to me that the climate was perfect; so Luther Merritte closed all the windows against the noise and dust and ushered me to one of those enormous leather armchairs that my bare lower arms and calves promptly stuck to.

"Now, then, while we are signing, shall I order in some coffee? My secretary brews a damn—darned good cup of coffee."

I had just eaten breakfast, but I was confused by his assumption that we were about to sign something—my will?—at once, and to stall for time, I agreed that I was dying for a good cup of coffee. He pressed a white button and the capable, middle-aged secretary left a pot of coffee on the end of Mr. Merritte's enormous desk.

We poured our own drinks and I started to ask him about the noisy project out the window but he reached into a desk drawer, brought out a manila folder and tossed it onto the desk. I didn't want to look at it. I knew perfectly well what it was: my last will and testament.

"Quite a simple matter, actually," he said, turning up the corner of each legal-sized page.

I said "mmm" and drank the hot coffee, fanning my mouth because, as usual, I had drunk before I tested the heat. I was angered at my stupidity in burning myself and this gave me the courage to announce firmly that I was not at all firm about the will.

"The trouble is," I said, "I know what I want to

do with the will, but I don't think I'm quite ready yet."

"Really!" His faint eyebrows went up against the bare, dome-like forehead. Clearly, I had taken him by surprise. "But it was my understanding . . . However, that is neither here nor there." He took the folder, tapped it unconsciously on the base of his desk-lamp. "Then, pardon me if I am indiscreet, Miss Tracey. Has something happened to change the provisions here? I was of the impression your father had submitted proofs of identity."

"Glenn Rivercombe seems to think I should be cautious. Of course, when it comes to proofs of identity, Mr. McKendrick's organization has provided all sorts of proof."

"Naturally, the fingerprints, that sort of thing. Your father was in the service in World War Two, I believe?"

"The Merchant Marine. But it isn't precisely that," I explained lamely. "I've gotten a kind of complex lately about making out this new will. I've never made one out before. And it depresses me. Makes me feel . . ."

With dawning comprehension, he began to look more cheerful. "Ah . . . I begin to see." His laugh was easy and gentle, directed not precisely at me, but apparently at all women. "That often happens. You mustn't feel that there is anything strange or —or weak about it. You take widows, for instance. They've had their menfolks to handle these legal matters all their lives. Comes time to do it themselves, they get cold feet, think it means they are going to drop dead. Actually, my dear, things have a habit of working out the opposite way. They make a will, they live forever. Practically."

I smiled. I had heard this somewhere before.

"I agree. Really, I do. The thing is—I suppose you could call it a superstition, but I felt funny about making things so definite. I'd rather do it later when I'm old. Forty or so. I mean . . ."

This time he did laugh at me.

"Forty or so. Judging by my own experience, it will arrive long before one is ready to admit it." He tapped the long, legal-sized folder absentmindedly. "The difficulty is—I'm afraid I must be brutally frank—life is uncertain. It is barely possible that through a sudden accident . . . Well, I needn't enumerate, but you will see that death is always with us. What about an illness? Or a fall in that lovely apartment of yours you inherited from your dear mother. Then, there are plane crashes. But I needn't go on. Much too depressing."

"It certainly is. You see, I'd like to just let things ride for a little while." But all his arguments were very telling. I had to admit they definitely influenced me. "However, if I signed this will, I could always change it; couldn't I?"

"Oh, absolutely. Codicils. Or, indeed, an entire

new will. But are you quite sure you wish to sign the will in its present state?"

What I wanted to do was to protect Father, in case one of those improbable things Mr. Merritte mentioned should happen to me. But I wanted also to leave the way open to change things in case Leah Chandragar or someone else with whom Father was involved should prove troublesome. Or dangerous? That seemed ridiculous in broad daylight, but probably wouldn't seem so impossible on another night so filled with uncertainties as last night.

I said slowly, "I believe I should sign now, but —is this sort of thing confidential?"

"Absolutely. It would be highly unethical to discuss the contents of a testament or, indeed, any legal matters conducted in these offices."

"Then, no one could call you up, let's say, and ask the contents of my will?"

He was so astonished I thought his eyebrows would remain fixed up on that domest forehead.

"My dear young lady! Never, to my knowledge, has such an indiscretion occurred. No legal firm of any probity at all could remain active in such circumstances."

"Okay. I'll sign tentatively. But later, I may put in some codicils. Or whatever."

Mr. Merritte turned the folder around, pulled out the blue-covered legal sheets enthusiastically, reminding me at the same time, "Since we are handling this matter for you rather than Rivercombe et cetera, we may assume you are to be—if I may say so—a lovely new addition to California's population."

That was going much too far, but I didn't argue with him. I waited until his secretary, a Notary Public, had entered the room, then I signed the several copies rapidly, because I didn't want to think about it.

Mr. Merritte smiled benevolently. "No, as we usually say at this point, 'You may die at any time, absolutely unworried. Your loved ones are perfectly protected.' "

I wrinkled my nose, but went on signing.

CHAPTER 5

I did not return to the hotel. It occurred to me that the longer I stayed away, the less likelihood there was of someone spying on me. But just to be sure, I went out the Market Street door and walked down to the Palace Hotel to get a cab. I wanted to give the name of some place far away as my destination, but this was only to avoid facing the mysteries surrounding my father. I liked being with him, but I was also curious. Did Leah Chandragar actually run his life? And what about those two called Chato and Verne?

No use in putting it off. Sooner or later I would have to satisfy my curiosity; allay my suspicions. There might even be something beyond curiosity and suspicion: simple, unpleasant jealousy. I had hoped to find my very own father. I had told myself he would likely have a life of his own, perhaps a family. Now that I had discovered that "family," I made up all these preposterous "suspicions" against them. Of course, I had a little help from Adam McKendrick!

"Fisherman's Wharf; the foot of Jones Street," I told the cab driver and we were off, presently climbing a hill so steep I shut my eyes momentarily and gritted my teeth. My stomach seemed to come up after me by several seconds. This was nothing compared to the trip down the hill, where the front wheels of all the parked cars were curbed, according to the law, and where the Golden Gate suddenly loomed up below us, the bridge towers afloat in the white fog.

Minutes later, we reached Jefferson Street, that wharfside thoroughfare whose name I had never noticed until yesterday. Indeed, I hadn't even known the street had a name. It was just "beside the wharf." Many of the famed restaurants and cafes, and most of the sideshow exhibits like Father's opened upon this street. The cab drove alongside Father's building.

"This it?"

"Yes. Fine, thank you." I started to get out.

"Nice place there. I mean—kind of interesting."

I looked over at the faded red brick wall. "I think so. My father owns it."

The cab driver studied the building in his rear-view mirror. "You don't say. Well, it's okay for my money. You learn a lot. Educational, you know. Now, me, I always got the *Titanic* mixed up with that boat that started us into World War One. That—you know the one."

"*Lusitania*?"

"That's the baby. I had some idea the Germans was hiding behind the icebergs and sunk the ship. Anyway, the wife and I took her niece and nephew. We had to go into every one. Cost us a fortune. Gave the wife such a case of jitters, she had to take one of them tranquilizers. You be careful, father or no father."

"Thank you. I will." He had brightened my day by his praise of Father's creation. I tipped him heavily, hoping I wasn't overdoing it so he'd think I was crazy.

Things were a little slow at this hour. Leah Chandragar was in the tight box office writing figures on a bright orange pad. I heard a shriek inside the building followed by giggles and laughter. Several couples were obviously having a great time suffering one or another form of shipwreck. Seeing me, Mrs. Chandragar shoved her note pad under the big red roll of tickets and flashed her enormously toothy smile. She crooked her finger toward me.

"Good morning, Barbara. Or is it afternoon? How good of you to come down here for lunch! But—what have you done with Tom?"

Surprised, I said, "I haven't seen him this morning. I've been away from the hotel."

"Oh, what a shame! He must have missed you. He said he was on his way to take you to lunch. Afterward he wants to show you around the docks. Have you ever walked out along that breakwater beyond Aquatic Park? Or the sailing vessels out there off the Hyde Street Pier?"

"No," I said and laughed apologetically for the confession. "What I have heard of is the Irish coffee at the Buena Vista. Anyway, I am sorry I missed Father." I knew I should stay and get better acquainted with Mrs. Chandragar, but she always made me feel uneasy. It was absurd, because she was being very kind, very enthusiastic, and I certainly had no reason to suspect her of insincerity; yet I found that when I looked at her, I wanted to shiver. It was wildly prejudiced and unfair.

She put out a graceful hand through the window in the glass.

"But you musn't go yet. You will so much disappoint poor Tom."

Searching for an excuse, I said lamely, "I do have a date this afternoon. Maybe I had better return to my hotel. Father will know how to contact me."

"No." She seemed a little anxious. Probably Father had made clear to her how much he wanted to be with his newly discovered daughter. Or would he do that? From the very beginning, had he been as anxious as I for this meeting?

"No, please wait, Barbara dear. I am certain he will be back at any time now. Or he will telephone. Either way, he will expect me to keep you here until he can get back."

I said lightly, "But not as a prisoner, I hope. And I do have several things to do."

Leah Chandragar was all reassurance. "Any minute. When he finds he has missed you, he will be back here in no time at all. Or he will call. Would you like to go in and explore?"

I looked around. There didn't seem to be anything of more pressing interest at the moment. Maybe this waiting period would give me a chance to know Mrs. Chandragar better, and indirectly to understand my father through his creative ability.

"I'd love to go in and see the exhibit, but to tell the truth, I have a perfectly ridiculous fear of heights. Do any of your exhibits have height problems?"

Mrs. Chandragar laughed good-humoredly.

"No, I am happy to say. There was some talk originally of having the *Titanic* exhibit take place in the crow's nest. The unfortunate lookouts were not issued binoculars, you know. And it seemed quite exciting for thrill-seekers to climb the rigging, pereh in that little crow's next, and see the foggy, misty scene clearing until—too late—they see the iceberg looming up before them."

I shivered. "Not my idea of thrill-seeking."

She held up her hand, swept away the idea. "No, no. The *Titanic* scene takes place in a cabin, as do the other scenes. More practical, you know."

No matter how she described it, it wasn't something I would enjoy, but I lied, "Yes, I'm sure it is."

"I'll call Chato to show you around."

"Please don't. I'll just wander over the exhibits." I remembered all too well that little man who had looked at me with such malevolence last night.

She shrugged. "As you like. You will find it educational. It is a pity you cannot enjoy the exhibits with someone you love. That is our slogan, you know: Scream With Someone You Love."

In the end she offered me a master-key and we argued over whether I should pay my way. She finally agreed that I could become a typical customer, using my own money. I had enough quarters for my purposes, the admission to each exhibit being fifty cents, after the original admission ticket. Anyway, I didn't intend to go through the agonies of four separate shipwrecks.

There was considerable noise inside the building. A roar and crackle punctuated by hideous screams.

"Morro Castle," Mrs. Chandragar called to me. "Customers are in there now. But your charming suit—too warm for that exhibit. I suggest you go to *Titanic*. First door on the right. That is cooler. Icebergs."

"Yes, I know." I went to the turnstyle, pressed the button and passed in to what was obviously a ship's passage. There were narrow passages immediately to the right and left with doors at the far end of these cross-halls. These led to the exhibit scenery, I assumed, and to the sound effects, all behind the exhibit cabins. The narrow cross-passages were intriguing, yet horrible, with all their noises of a ship fire. I went straight ahead. Beside the first cabin door was the neatly lettered sign on a polished brass plate: *RMS Titanic*. I backed away from the idea of suffering these horrors and found myself against the door opposite which seemed, to my vivid imagination, hot clear through. This was the *SS Morro Castle,* a ship about whose fire, which cost many lives, there were still questions after forty years, though it was now obvious the fire had been incendiary. In any case a large, noisy group was enjoying these thrills today. Behind the door, so oddly warm, I could hear over the crackle and roar of fire, the laughing shrieks of young thrill-seekers. I could also hear the voices of ship's officers issuing orders through the inferno. The voices were clearly panicked, which only made the bedlam worse.

It was not a "cabin" I wanted to enter. I walked down the cabin passage to the third and fourth doors. *Lusitania* was on the right and the *Andrea Doria* on the left. Neither ship had met a fate that attracted me, or even my curiosity. Beyond the last cabin there was another cross-passage and an interesting collection of scenic backdrops. A fifteen-watt light swung overhead. A flight of wooden steps, badly warped, led steeply up to the floor overhead, which appeared to be a gigantic loft. Someone was working up there. I could hear boxes being dragged, paper wadded up. Sound effects.

I laughed at my own uneasiness. Not that I was anxious to meet the surly Chato, but he was, at least, thoroughly accounted for up there. I wondered if he was also operating the rest of the machinery, voice and scream effects, for the ground-floor level where the customers were having such a good time being scared. I started to my right on the cross-passage, curious to see what the backdrops for *Titanic* and *Lusitania* looked like. But a crude door made of raw boards laced together by wire barred my way. It was barely relieved from darkness here in the corner by the faint glow from that small light about thirty feet away. I pushed against the boards, more or less experimentally, not expecting any results, but the door creaked open under my touch. The hasp and a cheap lock both hung loose, the hasp held by one screw. It was darker here, so dark that for a few seconds I couldn't see anything. I could eventually make out the cabin portholes of *Lusitania* nearest me and *Titanic* beyond, two portholes to each cabin. They faced these backdrops of raging seas, the slight, sharklike "fin" of a German U-Boat peering above the waves behind *Lusitania*'s portholes; and for *Titanic* just beyond, the ubiquitous iceberg which loomed up in curious, fascinating shades of ice-blue. The shades seemed to be luminous and faintly moving as if to embrace the viewer. Their illumination was controlled by the lighting from the exhibit interiors behind those portholes.

I moved along in a gingerly way, trying to figure out how all the endless technical details worked; for there appeared to be rollers and wheels and machinery under each of the two "cabins." A grinding sound started up, at first rather faint, then closer, and louder, much louder. A hideous crackling and the tearing of timbers, deafeningly loud in these narrow confines. I turned with difficulty, intending to retreat by the way I had squeezed in here, but somehow the *Lusitania* mechanism had been turned on. Apparently, inside the square shell of a room was the make-believe cabin and this, thanks to the mechanism underneath, was in the process of listing to a forty-five degree angle. The machinery was so close to me it caught at my suit skirt as I squeezed by in panic. I could see through the porthole that the cabin's objects were all fastened down, but to be inside that cabin would be like rolling around in a barrel.

The mechanism must have been rusted and poorly kept up, because it made hideous noises which had nothing to do with the sound track of a torpedoed ship. I took another step, and seeing something shoot out before my eyes, I ducked. A second later and I might have been beheaded by a steel girder that seemed to have snapped loose from the mechanism halfway up the wall of the container-cabin. One end of the steel fell to the floor with a terrific clatter and the mechanism stopped. Jammed, I supposed. I screamed and scrambled back to the cross-passage at the rear of the exhibit, slamming the old board door hard against the wall as I rushed out.

Something black suddenly got between me and the fifteen-watt light across the passage, a figure identifiable by his black hair and black jacket, all of which kept advancing and receding weirdly as the tiny light globe beyond swung back and forth.

I screamed as his gloved hands reached out. I tried to get around to pass him, recalling in a flash all the suspicions he had aroused in Adam McKendrick last night, and in me this morning when he entered the hotel restaurant. I couldn't take my eyes off those hands, surprisingly big for this young man of barely middle height, but then, he looked solid all over. I managed not to scream again while I complained furiously,

"I nearly died back there. Who turned that machinery on? I could have been killed."

"Then I guess the next order of the day is to find out what you were doing back there. It's no place for visitors, you know."

"Never mind that. Who are you? What do you want?"

"Look, beautiful! I ought to ask you that. These are my quarters. At least, I work here."

Suddenly, I realized what I should have suspected all the time.

"You are Verne! Mrs. Chandragar mentioned you." Whoever he was, it seemed very far-fetched that he should have turned on that mechanism and tried to kill me. It would have been so pointless. Besides, he might have killed me just now when I came out of that dark place beyond the cabins, if that was his mission in life. It had been an accident, that broken girder, but a dangerous one. It would teach me to mind my own business in future.

"Verne Chandragar. Right on," he said. "And I know you. You're Tom's long-lost daughter. You've been the chief topic of conversation around here the last week or so."

I took this opportunity to get around him and

back into the comparative freedom of the "ship's passage."

"You could hardly have failed to know me," I pointed out. "You have been following me all over town."

"Me!" Then he laughed. "You mean this morning? That was kind of an accident. I figured you'd have breakfast in your suite. I sure would if I had your money, sister."

"Sister!"

"Figure of speech." Seeing my expression he nodded toward the far end of the passage and the turnstyle leading to the box office. "That's Mother. I think she's got some notion to help the old man by making me irresistible to you. Figures Tom and I might both make a haul off you."

"Dead or alive?" I asked him caustically.

He stared. "Are you really afraid of me?"

"Certainly not!" I lied. "I can't wait any longer for Father. You might tell him that when he comes back."

"Look here." He reached for me but I eluded him. He followed along the passage. "You've got me wrong. No kidding, Miss Tracey. I've got your interest at heart. Just like that private eye you've been leaning on so much. That McKendrick's no better than me when it comes to looking after you."

I thought this was uproariously funny, and was

about to tell Verne Chandragar as much when the cabin door of the *Morro Castle* exhibit flew open and five teen-agers poured out, screaming with glee, and a dose of hysteria.

"I'm seasick!" one of the leaders yelled. "Looka me! I'm heavin'!" Everyone pushed after him and they rushed out into the salt air sweeping in off the Golden Gate.

As I was passing the *Morro Castle* door, which was still ajar, I saw a snatch of the cabin. There were two bunks, permanent sets with upper bunks above. The room had a thin, worn piece of carpeting and the meager furnishings were of a dark, depressing color, including the dresser, the bathroom door and the double closet. Whatever thrills there had been were turned off now. The cabin looked dull, unexciting, except for what had happened in its original in the early thirties, to a ship full of carousing tourists eluding the Prohibition restrictions of mainland United States. A crowd that had laughed and joked and drunk clear up to the time the inferno burst upon them!

Verne slammed the door, which locked at once. He explained as I looked back curiously, "Some of the kids like to use these bunks for a love-in. We have to shoo 'em out every once in a while."

Now that we were out in the daylight of the Wharf, I saw that young Chandragar was totally unlike the frightful fiend of my imagination. Nothing could be more harmless than that easy, friendly grin of his, the grin of a child who hasn't yet discovered right from wrong. I tried to keep that in mind.

I didn't know what to make of him. If he was going to be dangerous, he had plenty of opportunity there in the back of the cabin exhibit. Yet he had done nothing, been kind and helpful and friendly. A person one could trust. Perhaps, after all, I had two people I could trust in San Francisco: Adam McKendrick and Verne Chandragar. But his name reminded me of his mother, and there I balked. I couldn't see myself trusting her. Everything in me revolted at the idea that she was sincere.

"Here we are, safe and sound," Verne called to his mother, who had started out of the box office as if startled to see us together, and both perfectly safe. Or was that, too, my heated imagination?

"Good. How fortunate you met each other! I've been expecting your father, Barbara. I can't imagine what is delaying him."

That wasn't the only mystery. I still wondered why Mrs. Chandragar's son had been chasing all over San Francisco following Adam and me. He seemed utterly indifferent to Father's whereabouts.

"How about me taking you to lunch, Miss Tracey? And you, Mother?" he suggested as if nothing in the world would please him more.

"My dear child," his mother reminded him in the voice of a strict but fair schoolteacher, "If I go to lunch with you, who remains to mind the store? You saw what happened last night. Or did you?"

He laughed and shrugged. "Ma, you know Chato. He was always lousy with figures."

"To his own advantage. Run along, Verne. Take Barbara to the Franciscan. Or Sabella's. Tourists adore them, Barbara dear. And the food is good. Then come back. Tom is sure to be here by then."

I began to make objections, not at all sure I wanted to spend so much time in Verne Chandragar's company. I had a feeling he was his mother's little black-haired helper, trying to occupy my time, or maybe even get me to like him, in order to help her in some way. The trouble was, I didn't know what her purpose could be.

At that minute I found myself very much under the malign gaze of the ugliest man I had ever seen. It was Chato. Something was wrong with the poor man's back. He moved in a huddled manner with his back bowed, and I tried not to think of the anthropoids he resembled. He paid little attention to Mrs. Chandragar or her son. He pointed a hand at me.

"I saw you sneakin' about back there. Spyin' around our property. I saw you."

I felt like saying rudely, "So you tried to kill

me!" but I managed to ignore him and to try again to get out of the lunch with Verne Chandragar.

Mrs. Chandragar said impatiently, "Chato, shut up! Now, Barbara my dear, don't be difficult. You must know it is my—Tom's and my dearest wish that you two children should become friends. Run along now."

Good heavens! I thought. The woman was trying to drum up a romance between her son and Tom Tracey's daughter. I could have laughed at the hopelessness of that. For all his open innocence, his boyish grin, Verne Chandragar was still the sinister, black-clad fellow who had followed me all over town in the most sneaky way, and for no conceivably good reason.

Soon, however, I began to think a quiet, pleasant lunch with something to warm my fear-chilled body might be just the treatment I needed.

"Why not? Let's go. And, Mrs. Chandragar, try and keep Father here until we return."

"Certainly, my dear. Run along, children. And have a good time."

"Mother the matchmaker," Verne remarked, with sardonic humor as we walked toward the famed restaurants of Fisherman's Wharf.

I was startled by his frankness and wondered if he was as repulsed by the whole idea of his mother's conniving as I was. I pretended to ignore his comment.

"How long has Mrs. Chandragar known my father?" I asked abruptly.

He shrugged. "Oh—years. I was up in the country going to school when I first heard about it. Your dad was looking for financing."

"Sounds like Father."

"I figured him for a drifter, putting the clutch on Ma. She was running the fortune-telling bit just off the Wharf."

This struck me as funny and I said so; since we were being so frank.

"And here I thought all this time that your mother was trying to get what she could out of Father. Maybe it was the reverse."

To my surprise he agreed very easily. "Sounds like Ma. She staked old Tom when he started the ship gimmicks. So she'd sure as hell want to stick around for any goodies he can squeeze out of you."

"Dead or alive?" I repeated myself, but I had begun to think a lot about this in the last twenty-four hours.

He stopped for a minute, while tourists piled up behind us. "What's that supposed to mean?"

"Simply that I was nearly brained—or beheaded—a little while ago, just before I met you. You must have thought I acted very oddly when I walked into you in back of the exhibits. But I was just plain scared."

"Got to admit I don't usually get that reception when a doll falls into my arms." As we went up the stairs of the glass-enclosed Franciscan Restaurant on the edge of the Bay, he glanced at me, frowning. "But what about the beheading, or whatever?"

I figured it would do me no harm to let him know I was on my guard and suspected everyone. I told him about the broken steel and the wholly unexpected operation of the *Lusitania* cabin.

The headwaiter, meeting us at the top of the stairs, unfortunately kept Verne from replying to me at once. It was not until we were seated and had given our order that he answered my repeated question: "Well, what do you think of it?"

"Think of what? Ever see a view like that? That's Alcatraz out there."

"I recognize it from old George Raft movies. Don't evade the issue. Do accidents often happen like the one that I just missed behind the *Lusitania* cabin?"

"Not often, but sometimes. You know, the weirdo thing is, when I was a kid, I didn't like this town. Now, I wouldn't live anywhere else."

"How often do they happen, exactly?"

"How often does what happen?"

Was he being deliberately dense? "Accidents! With the cabin machinery."

He was definitely hesitant. "Now and again.

Like during a dock strike a year or so ago. This scab—well, he was more of a spy—was making trouble on the *Embarcadero*. Bunch got after him and he hightailed it along the Wharf to the exhibit. He hid behind the *Doria* cabin. Some of us chased after him. He panicked and crawled under the *Doria* cabin. Then something happened." He stopped talking to take a long drink of ice water.

No question. He was nervous. But I was pretty anxious myself. "Go on. Go on! Something happened."

"The—the machinery started up. It got turned on accidentally. That's the only way it figured to happen. Maybe one of the gang chasing him just stuck some quarters in the slot . . . nobody would ever admit it. Anyway, the exhibit was closed down for a few weeks until they decided it was . . . an accident." He drank again, looked out the window at the windswept bay. "He was pretty badly mutilated. Made you kind of sick to think about the whole exhibit afterward. But you forget these things after a while. Anyway, there was some thought maybe I'd done it. Well, it's about forgotten now, I hope."

I couldn't help the sarcasm in my voice: "And does the machinery break down very often? Or only when it is absolutely necessary?"

His black eyes stared at me, "drilled me" would describe it better.

"You think you're pretty cute; don't you? The benevolent Miss Tracey! You and that eye, McKendrick. Well, he may not be as tough as he thinks he is, running around like your armoured guard!"

I felt distinctly cold, and my smile was a real effort.

"Is this a threat?"

"No," he said grimly. "Just a little advice. You may find you need more than that big brave eye to protect you."

"Meaning you?"

"You could do worse."

CHAPTER 6

I should have been grateful for the lunch. The poached salmon with egg sauce was mouthwatering, and Verne's scallops, golden brown and not overcooked, looked equally tempting. All the time we were eating, Verne gazed moodily at his plate and I stared at the Golden Gate, at the red-and-white excursion boat slipping into its dock, and at the green hills on the Marin County horizon. I can't imagine what he was thinking, but I know I was seriously wondering if Verne Chandragar had operated the *Lusitania* mechanism today in order to get me out of the way. After all, if I died, his mother's lover, Tom Tracey, would inherit over a million dollars.

He certainly wasn't crazy about Adam McKendrick. The first subject he brought up near the end of our lunch was "That eye . . . you better take some good advice and look a couple of times at that guy before you trust him any further."

"Thanks," I said. "I'll remember."

It was curious, all the same. I could almost believe him at certain moments, like this.

We both made an effort to be sociable on the way back to the museum, pretending nothing deadly had been said or hinted at between us. I had no notion whether my companion was surprised when we reached Mrs. Chandragar in the box office, but I certainly was surprised to find my father had not arrived yet; nor had he been heard from.

The museum was filled with customers. All four ships' cabins were operating and there was considerable racket that reached the turnstyle and box office. I glanced in before remarking to Mrs. Chandragar, "I hope your *Lusitania* exhibit has been shored up. It was falling apart when I was back there an hour or two ago."

Leah Chandragar looked a trifle surprised, as well she might, if she was innocent. She gave me the full benefit of her toothy smile. "It has worked perfectly until now, with no complaints. As a matter of fact, *Lusitania* has been quite busy ever since you left."

I couldn't resist the dig: "Of course, it may have

been only for my benefit that it produced the guillotine effect." I punctuated this with a dry and not too successful laugh. "See you again, no doubt. And—Verne, you must let me repay your hospitality sometime soon. I'll give you a call. Maybe we can have dinner at the hotel. Or wherever."

"Thank our dear Barbara!" his mother commanded sharply, but I didn't wait to hear Verne's response. I walked away, followed by Mrs. Chandragar's voice, "When your father returns, where shall I say you have gone?"

"Tell him to call my hotel and leave a message," I called to her, and walked up the hill, hoping to hail a cab. As is often the case, there were none to be had, and in the end, I went to the turntable and caught the Hyde Street Cable Car as it headed upward.

This time, by dint of holding on tight, and opting for the best while fearing the worst, I managed to make the journey up hill, over crests, around corners and down the steep Powell Street slope to my hotel on Union Square.

There was a telephone message for me in my suite. I called to check and found it was not from my father, as I had expected, but from Adam McKendrick. In a sense, though I liked Adam, I was disappointed. Or maybe just uneasy. If Father had come to see me, surely he would have left a message. And if he hadn't come here, why had he lied to Leah Chandragar?

I called Adam at his office and left my name with his secretary. The girl was surprised.

"But Miss Tracey, I understood Mr. McKendrick would be seeing you and your father today. He called in half an hour ago and said he was on the track of something. I thought he meant that he had found you. Or your father, I'm not sure which."

"If he has," I said, "he's luckier than his friends and I have been. My father was expected here, but he doesn't seem to have arrived." I laughed, trying to pass off my remark as a joke. "Since Father and Adam have both disappeared, maybe they've disappeared together."

Her laugh was distinctly hollow. "That would be funny. Frankly, Miss Tracey, there is very little likelihood. I have a feeling, only a feeling, mind—that Mr. McKendrick had been on a new investigation. He sounded . . . disturbed when he checked in, though he didn't explain."

"All right. Just say I called."

What on earth did this new development mean? Then it occurred to me that Adam had many cases. Mine was settled, more or less to his satisfaction, and now he was working on another case. Nevertheless, I kept getting odd notions all afternoon, twinges of worry; sudden, sharp fears: *Something is wrong and no one will tell me what it is.*

Common sense came to my rescue immediately

after, and I went on reading or watching television, or writing to friends in Chicago. When the telephone rang late in the day, I jumped nervously, as if I had never again expected to hear that buzzing sound. It was Adam McKendrick. He had the nerve to begin by saying, "You're certainly hard to get hold of, young lady."

"I don't know why," I said snappishly. "I've been here all afternoon."

That took the wind out of his sails. Somewhat mollified, he half-apologized.

"I see. I haven't called since one-thirty. One or two things came up and I've been bird-dogging it all over the Bay Area ever since. . . . By the way, you haven't heard from your father this afternoon; have you?"

"Not yet. He was coming to see me around noon today."

"And he never showed?"

For some reason I felt it necessary to defend Father, although it wasn't clear to me precisely what was so wrong about his having changed his mind, or being called away. It wasn't as though he had made a definite date with me.

"But I wasn't here when Father came to see me. By the time I reached the hotel, he had gone. You can't expect him to hang around here for hours waiting for a daughter. A girlfriend, maybe. But a daughter—?"

"A rich daughter."

"You spend an awful lot of time thinking about money!"

He laughed, quite unruffled. "That's right. I meant to tell you, we received our company check from your Chicago people in the morning mail; so your credit is restored. Want to open a new account with McKendrick and Company?"

"No, thank you. I have no more business with private eyes."

There was a little silence. I wondered if I should hint that there were other relationships besides business, and then, for a few heartbeats, I had the odd notion that he had been about to answer me with something serious, but he changed his mind. "You might, after all, have more. Look here, Barby, must it all be business? How about pleasure with your private eye? Say, dinner tonight. I can afford it, now that our biggest account has paid us off."

I was delighted at the whole idea of a cheerful evening with the attractive and usually good-humored Adam McKendrick. I needed something of this sort. I had been depressed all day, and aside from the accident with that mechanical contraption, there wasn't any definite reason for it. I must be sure and tell Adam about the "accident." Maybe he could do a little snooping, or have someone discover whether the *Lusitania*'s broken steel bar had really been an accident.

"I'd love to," I said quickly. "I'll be big about this thing and let you use up your Tracey fee on me. Sort of . . . get my money back by foul means."

He chuckled. "I'll take that chance. Look, it's the devil to find a parking place around there, so can I pick you up in front of the hotel?"

"I knew it," I sighed. "I'm being taken for granted already. . . . What time?"

He was amused at my joke, but I couldn't get over the feeling that he was forcing himself to this light mood.

"I thought I'd kidnap the heiress. Smuggle her out of the city and over to a snug little steakhouse I know in Marin County. What do you say?"

"An heiress? Anybody I know? Great! I'll help you. What's the ransom to be?"

This time I couldn't help hearing the real warmth in his voice as he promised, "We'll work that out later. How about six-thirty?"

"I'll have the victim ready for delivery on the dot."

"Good. I knew I could count on my favorite client."

I was about to hang up when he added in that now-familiar, troubled tone, "And Barby . . . would you promise me something?"

"Of course. I'll bring my checkbook."

He didn't play up to this. "Don't make any

more dates. Remember! With anyone." He pretended to laugh, but I knew it for a pretense. "I'm the jealous type. Or hadn't you noticed?"

"All Don Juans are," I informed him, and we both hung up after good byes.

I set the phone back thoughtfully. I doubted very much if his so-called jealousy had anything to do with his command to me. It was something else. My instincts had been right. He was seriously concerned about something, and whatever it might be, it was connected with Barbara-Jane Tracey. Was it for this reason that Adam decided to "kidnap" me across the Golden Gate, to get me out of reach of someone tonight?

Whatever his reason, I wasn't going to turn down the invitation. I was blue enough already with my own company.

While I was dressing for the kidnap-dinner, the telephone buzzed. I crossed the bedroom, wondering and uneasy. But it had taken me a minute or two to reach the telephone beside my bed and when I took the phone off the cradle, I heard the little, dry click as the party on the other end of the line rang off. I had a fierce, driving compulsion to talk to that party and I couldn't have explained it, even to myself. It was just a terrible feeling that I should have answered, that it was important. I kept calling "Hello!" but it was too late.

I went back to finish dressing, counting hopefully on the cut of my sleeveless black sheath which I brightened with a flame-red scarf and a pin with an ecological message: a gold fox in a red jacket and red hunter's cap. A bushy-tailed fox aiming his long-barreled gold rifle, obviously, at mankind. I wore pumps, unfashionable that year, because their heels were high and narrow. But they displayed my ankles and legs to the best advantage, and I felt I needed all the help I could get in dealing with the man Glenn Rivercombe had called a "Don Juan."

I arrived in front of the hotel five minutes early. The elegant doorman started to signal for a taxi, but I shook my head, and almost in answer to this gesture, Adam McKendrick drove up in a yellow Chrysler, honked for me and got out to play the gentleman and help me in. The doorman beat him to it, though, and we drove off in record time.

"Remarkable girl!" Adam said a minute or two later.

"Really? How so? Tell me more."

"You were on time. Very rare trait."

It was not precisely a compliment that I could take to my heart and memory. I remarked with an edge to the words, "I was before time. Even more rare." As he looked at me, I added, "It was an accident. Nothing planned about it."

"Too bad." He had a funny, crooked grin whose charm grew on me. I knew I had better watch myself or I'd be as lost as Mr. Rivercombe's blonde client who had come to Adam for evidence against an unwanted husband.

He headed for Van Ness Avenue, turned off on Lombard, and in a few minutes we were headed across the Golden Gate Bridge, under a blaze of sunset so piercing and gaudy I wouldn't have believed it in a technicolor movie. Adam pointed out the sunset to me, and the curious way it had of making the Bay waters look aflame. He talked a great deal, and while I enjoyed his conversation and his company, I began to suspect that he really was trying to keep both our minds off the subject that had brought us together in the first place—Father's identity.

When we were cutting through the Marin Hills, now shadowed, I asked him suddenly, "What happened today?" I wanted to broach the subject of my own adventure, but thought it just might have something to do with the problem that clearly occupied him.

"What the devil do you mean?" He must have had something definite on his mind, or he wouldn't have been so curt, so abrupt.

"Something happened. Was it about my father? I've felt sure it was, ever since you called this afternoon."

He was concentrating on the highway, evidently looking for a turnoff.

"I have several cases, my dear girl. They don't all involve you, even if you are the prettiest."

Offended, I said nothing and looked out the window until we made a turn onto a small country road, tree-lined and smelling of eucalyptus and drying grass. I lowered the window and leaned out. In spite of all my efforts to keep quiet, I couldn't resist exclaiming, "You weren't joking when you talked about kidnapping me. This is pretty desolate country."

"Only five minutes from the main highway." But he did smile. Then he shook me a little by staring hard into the rear-view mirror. I turned to see what it was that attracted his attention.

I saw a large, old black Cadillac bumping along behind us, in which I could make out a white-haired man at the wheel and another middle-aged man beside him. Two women were in the back seat. One leaned forward to speak with the driver.

"Good heavens!" I said. "One of those women is wearing a fur coat, I think."

This remark, so unimportant to Adam in his present tension, made him laugh.

"A non-sequitur, but perfectly true."

"I wonder if they are headed for the same place. And if not, just where they are going on this road?"

"It's a popular enough steakhouse. They look authentic."

I remarked with satirical humor, "Not hired killers, or international spies, you mean."

His free hand closed over mine. If there is a difference in the touch of one male hand which may have been very like other male hands in the past, then I certainly felt the difference in this one. Not the warmth, or the size, but a certain chord that produced recognition and response in me. I felt like a child of eight, holding hands with my first boyfriend. Only the vibrations between Adam and me were stronger. I hated to break the chord of this moment but there was still the matter of the *Lusitania* machinery to discuss with him. I brought it up now.

"I was almost killed today."

His hand tightened its grip, so tightly I winced. "How did it happen?"

I explained how I had walked behind those exhibit cabins just in time to have a loose steel girder —"Well, not quite a girder, say a bar"—rammed out from the exhibit. "It missed me by a hair."

"Thank God for that, anyway."

He glanced at me, then back at the road ahead. We were approaching an unpaved parking lot bordered on one side by a long wooden shack that looked like—and probably had been—an oldtime bunkhouse. Why is it that all the best eating places have to be so disreputable-looking? But all the same, I liked it. For one thing, wood smoke was pouring out of the chimney; and the marvelous, acrid odor suggested camping, delicious dinners over the coals on long-ago trips, and joy without worry.

Adam must have guessed how the wood smoke affected me, or else he shared the sensation of wonderful nostalgia, because when we had parked and gotten out of the car, he put his arm around me, and pulled me close as we walked along the rocky path to the screen door of the old bunkhouse.

"S-T-E-A-K-S" said the badly painted sign over the doorway. Nothing else. Just "STEAKS." I thought this made it more cozy and the steaks more succulent.

Behind us the four in the Cadillac drove up, parked. The two men got out, still talking business between themselves and started along the path after us. I whispered to Adam, "They certainly care a lot about their wives." The two stout women came along in their wake, likewise chattering busily.

Adam grinned and a little of his worry seemed to lift briefly. "Old married couples."

I shuddered. "Horrible example. They almost cure me."

"Have you thought about it? I mean—you aren't engaged, or anything?"

"There's a joke attached to that but I won't fall into it. I'm not currently engaged. As for *anything* —I won't commit myself."

He startled me by asking suddenly, "How did you get along with young Chandragar?"

"Fine. So far as I know. Who told you about Verne?"

He brushed this aside as a tiresome detail.

"Never mind that. Did he try anything?"

Was he jealous? That would be promising. Before I could make anything out of it, however, he pursued his dislike of Verne Chandragar and destroyed any faint hopes I might have that there was something personal in his curiosity.

"You've probably guessed that the whole business of this fellow's play for you is being maneuvered by his mother."

I looked at him with sickening adoration. "You make me feel so—wanted."

The screen door shrieked closed behind us. We were expected. A huge female, taller and brawnier than Adam himself, nodded to us in greeting and motioned us to follow her across the rickety board floor, between tables with blue-and-white checked tablecloths, to the bar, a long, narrow, alley-like addition to the restaurant, made narrower by the lengthy bar and stools. Two bearded, talkative young men were drinking at the far end of the bar. They seemed to be deep in an argument and paying no attention to us, but Adam eyed them suspiciously before we took stools at the opposite end of the bar.

When Adam had placed our order with the lean

and spry little barman, he asked me at once, "About this accident at the museum today? Who was there at the time?"

I explained about Chato working overhead. Or was that Verne Chandragar? I never had been quite sure. I knew only that both were in the building and Leah was outside.

"And Tom Tracey? Where was he?"

"Certainly not in the museum." I reminded him that Father had very likely been in my hotel, calling for me, at that time, but I could see Adam's doubt.

He started to say so when the fat foursome from the black Cadillac crowded into the bar and managed to straddle the center bar stools. Since they were clearly minding their own business, Adam continued to me, "I have reasons, good reasons, believe me, Barby, why I think we've made a ghastly mistake. That is why I asked you to trust me. Just for a day or so, until we can verify something." I started to speak but he put two fingers on my lips. I decided curiosity could wait. I didn't like to break this mood or his warm smile that went with it. "Promise?"

Being unable to talk, I nodded. He leaned over, removed his fingers and kissed me softly, but firmly. It was unfortunate that the little barman delivered our drinks in the middle of this.

The fat lady nearest us began to giggle and buzzed away in whispers with her companions.

Adam scowled in their direction and began to drink his Scotch.

"Is it really so bad?" I asked presently, in a half-whisper.

He made an effort. "Not bad at all, actually. Just my way of getting you to myself for a few hours." I watched his wry, slightly lopsided smile appear as he added, "I can't spend my life wrestling young Chandragar for your company."

This reminded me of Verne's antagonism and I mentioned it. "He spent most of our lunch date warning me against you. Are your astrological signs crossed or something like that?"

"Something like that. Drink up. I have a feeling our conversation is proving irresistible to our neighbors."

"Righto, Captain!" I was rapidly feeling better as it began to seem that Adam really was jealous. If all this interest in me was part of his job, and only his job, it would have been an awful letdown.

We lingered over dinner at the old square tables with the blue-checked cloths. Adam had been right about the steaks. They were well-aged, juicy and tender, and much too big for me. There were baked potatoes heavy with sour cream and chives, which Adam despised, and a green salad. I had to leave half of everything. But the best part of dinner was our long, close conversation which did not once touch on the curious "dangers" which seemed to surround me. We talked mostly about our ideas of love, sex, marriage—we were both skeptics—and male-female relationships. It was one of those lovely, intimate times when expectation is everything, and where we came to know each other emotionally, to enjoy each other's presence without the usual fears, reservations, or sudden feelings of doubt. We liked each other.

Late in the evening, during which time other customers had come and gone, I knew I had to revert to the unpleasant subject that had brought us together tonight.

"Adam . . . can't you tell me now? What really is the thing you've been worried about all day?"

He had been stroking my fingers as I questioned him and it was difficult to concentrate on serious matters while that special, massaging touch of his was operating at full power.

"About now. About this." He raised my fingers. It was hard to ignore the special look in his eyes. Curiously enough, all my life I had a passion for dark eyes. Looking into his eyes now, that quite electrifying blue, I was amazed at my bad taste of former years.

"I'm not going to get a direct answer, am I?" I rather hoped I wasn't, now.

He was delightfully gentle. "No, my darling. Not just yet." I forgave a good deal for that "darling," so different from the brisk pseudo-friendship of the "darlings" among my usual friends.

"I think maybe we'd better be getting back," I said finally. "Do you realize it's nearly eleven? You have an office to go to tomorrow, I suppose. Or aren't you an office man?"

"Men with beautiful secretaries are always office men."

I made a face at the idea, wondering at my own proprietary thoughts about him. He laughed then and surprised me by discounting the "beautiful secretary" bit. "One thing most business men discover very early: not to hire beautiful secretaries. They're too distracting. I regard my girl Friday as extremely attractive and extremely efficient. She regards me as her cranky boss. Believe me, the ideal arrangement! . . . Well, I guess this is as good a time as any. We won't need to kill any more time. I can get you safely tucked in now."

I had a sudden, distinct feeling that this lovely evening had been purely business, after all. His job was to protect his client and he had done so, even if he had to get personal to do so.

"Let's go," I said abruptly. "You're right. I've got to be tucked in."

As we left and drove back across the Golden Gate, he persisted in trying to bring the conversation back to the personal, to light romance and flattery, but it was too late. To me, the letdown had been great. Or maybe I had felt too deliciously high, falsely secure in the thought that this good-looking, popular man felt something a little special for me.

Eventually, when we were approaching our destination in front of the hotel, Adam lost his friendly, teasingly romantic air.

"Are you angry with me?"

I said, "Certainly not. Frankly, I owe you a great deal for tonight. Maybe my life. At least, I get that feeling."

Instead of arguing, he looked distractingly grim.

"You may be right. I hope to God you aren't. Here we are."

The doorman opened the door just as Adam was reaching for me. I eluded Adam's hands and stepped out to the sidewalk. I waved behind me without looking around. As a matter of fact, I needn't have bothered to look around to know that Adam gunned his motor and roared off in what was either a terrible hurry or a terrible temper. I had the desolate consolation of knowing I had succeeded in seeming immune to his celebrated charm.

Depressed and angry, I crossed the long, high-ceilinged lobby and headed for the red-padded elevator.

"Might as well be in a padded cell," I complained to myself, only to find I was sharing the elevator with a short, stout white-haired old lady with a mouth full of false teeth.

"Dear me," she murmured politely, "do you think so?"

This made me laugh in spite of my disappointment over the outcome of my romantic evening. I was still smiling when I reached the door of my suite and heard the telephone buzzing inside. I turned the key in the lock quickly and hurried in. I had the faint hope it might be Adam McKendrick.

I reached for the sitting-room phone. I remember how hopeful, how thrilled I sounded: "Hello?"

Someone on the other end of the line took a sharp breath.

"Barby dear? This is Tom . . . This is your father."

He was out of breath, or ill. At any rate, something was wrong.

CHAPTER 7

I asked anxiously, "Is something wrong? Where are you, Father?"

"Sprout . . . I guess you'd say I'm in trouble. Look here. Don't beat around the bush. Do you feel anything for me at all? Anything?"

I was bewildered. "Of course, I do. Daddy, you know when I was little, we got on lots better than I did with Mother. I always felt I understood you. Even when we were apart. Maybe—maybe I'm like you in some ways."

"No, honey. Don't bother with the blarney. That's not what I need."

I felt a little sick with disappointment. I moistened my lips and made myself sound hearty and cheerful.

"You need some money." I wanted to give him plenty, a large sum, maybe in trust, an annuity so he would always have plenty. But this was so quick, hardly more than twenty-four hours since our reunion. Was tonight a time for learning ugly truths from everyone?

"Money?" He sounded vague, as if his mind were wandering. "Well, later, maybe. I don't know. I'm kind of mixed up right now. Haven't worked anything out. God! What a headache!" He laughed, a funny, wry laugh. "I guess there is something you could do for me. I could sure use a couple of aspirin."

"Father! Where are you?"

"I'm only a block away from you. Only a block. Might as well be on the moon. I can't explain over the phone. Tell you what it is. Now I think of it, I could use a few bucks. Do you have a little ready cash, honey?"

"I think I could get it. How much?" I wondered how many hundreds, or more likely thousands, he needed. I was astonished by his answer.

"Twenty bucks. Thirty at the most. Just 'til I get to my safe deposit box. I've got a little salted away. But I want to explain things to you. I've got to make you understand."

I almost cut off his last words to urge him, "Come up now. And tell me all about it. Of course, I'll understand. I'm your daughter."

There was a small silence, but not a complete silence. I could hear his heavy, anxious breathing. Then he said haltingly, "Honey, if I could . . . But don't you see? I don't dare leave here. I'll be seen. Anywhere along the street. It could be anybody. I wouldn't even know 'em by the looks. Could you—I've been thinking. Girls wear lots of wigs and things these days. You wouldn't have brought some wigs with you, by any lucky chance?"

"Wigs!" I glanced at the closet. My wig box was on the floor among my other luggage. "I did bring one wig. It's streaked blonde, kind of a shag cut. I don't think you'd like me in it. It's not a wig that fathers would approve of. I only wear it when I want to be devastatingly sophisticated."

I had some wild, preposterous idea that he wanted to borrow my wig for some masquerade. He completely threw me by his fervent plea: "Good! You don't look like yourself in it. How about clothes? You got any clothes you haven't worn here in the city?"

"I think so. Yes. Of course. Look here, Father, do you want me to disguise myself, or something? What are you doing? One of Adam McKendrick's private-eye jobs?"

"No! And, Sprout, I don't want him to know a thing about this. It's—well, it's pretty important to me."

He sounded frightened. There seemed to be no doubt of his sincerity. "You want me to get myself up as this blonde buzz-bomb and meet you? At this hour? It's almost midnight."

"But only a block, honey. You're my last hope. There's not another living soul I can trust. Remember. Corner bar. The MARQUEE. I'll be in the rear banquette, across from the piano. It's kind of dark there now. Not much business. And—can you wear different shoes? Or do anything to make yourself different? Your walk? Anything?"

"I understand."

"God! I—I was afraid you might let me down. Honey, I should never have let you go back when you were a kid. But it's too late. I'll be waiting for you, Sprout."

After I set the phone back, I stood there a minute in a kind of stupor. The whole thing was idiotic, but I knew I had to do it. If there was one fact I would risk my life on—and maybe I was doing just that—it was Father's very real fear.

I rummaged through my closet, decided at this hour the more unobtrusive I looked, the better. I could be a girl headed for a trolley-bus on Market Street after an evening shift at one of the restaurants. I got out my golf shoes. A girl who stood on her feet a lot ought to wear comfortable shoes after hours. They were terribly unflattering, but flattery wasn't the object tonight.

I changed to a dark slack suit I would never wear in town, certainly not in San Francisco which, even in these benighted days, was the best-dressed city in the country. I got out the streaked blonde wig, pinned it on over my dark hair, combing the wig into some kind of dishevelled order. Just to make doubly sure none of my dark tendrils were visible, I took a brown and rust scarf and tied it over the wig, babushka-style. I did look awfully tacky. Taking a deep breath, I started for the door, then decided to arm myself with a weapon of sorts: a long, sharp Thai letter-opener. I put this up my sleeve with the point protruding just beyond the nail of my middle finger. I completed the wardrobe with a beach-bag in place of a handbag, and started out.

The halls were deserted. The elevator, too. In the long lobby on the street floor a convention was breaking up, but not a soul seemed to notice me. I went out a side exit, unobtrusive, trying to look a little tired, a little cross after a hard evening's work. From my reflection in a showcase I could see that I succeeded all too well. I almost failed to recognize myself with the blonde wig, the depressingly tied scarf, and those shoes.

I crossed the street and started down the block Father had mentioned. It was cold with the moist and biting embrace of white fog curling around those of us who had to be out at this hour. The Square, now behind me, was deserted, with that pregnant stillness that suggests sleeping. There was no one on the street who looked sinister, ominous, interested in me or my father. Every loner I saw was bustling along somewhere. The pairs dragged their feet, walked close, hands in each other's pockets to keep warm, intent on nothing, it seemed, except getting each other to bed.

I hurried along, past three bars in the one block, past solitary males who glanced at me without excitement, and dully looked away. Then I saw the sign MARQUEE, on the corner bar ahead. I had never found it necessary to hang around bars alone, but this one looked harmless and I found myself surprised at its respectability. A series of psychedelic lights operated in back of the long bar like tiny Christmas Tree lights. Several men and one woman sat at the bar. An elderly man and a very young, rather hard-looking blonde were cuddled together in the first banquette, near the door.

I walked in. I felt odd, uncertain. I didn't belong. I felt intrusive. One of the men at the bar looked around, nudged another man. Their faces were eerie blobs in the little flashes of light behind the bar.

"Drink, sister?" the first one asked me.

I ignored him. To my surprise they left me alone. I passed them, walking close to the banquettes, as far from the bar as possible. There was a grand piano at the far end of the room, beyond the bar. Opposite it was the last banquette. The banquette was empty.

A door opened at the rear. Probably the toilets

were back there. An attractive brunette woman about thirty-five came out. I must have looked pretty confused because she came to me and asked politely, "May I help you?"

I said eagerly, "Yes. I was to meet someone in that booth. A middle-aged man, tall, with graying hair. Irish. Very . . . Irish."

Her smile began slowly, but it was not a malicious smile. "Not . . . a gentleman friend."

"No, no. My father. But he's very attractive. Did you see him? He might have been a little . . . nervous."

She nodded. "He asked to use the phone about half an hour ago. As you say, he had charm. He didn't want to use the public phone in front. So I suggested he use the one in my office."

I looked around. I lost some of my nervousness. Maybe everything was all right, after all. Father would pop out of some dark corner and explain things, and I devoutly hoped my arrival would save him from whatever troubles had him so terrified.

"Where is he now?"

The woman followed my searching gaze. "That's funny. He came back out here, ordered a beer, and—never mind. I'll find out from Bruno. He'll know. You sit back here where you can be comfortable. How would you like a—let's say—a grasshopper while you wait. That's a light one, with creme de menthe."

She was treating me like a child. Apparently my blonde wig and the rest hadn't produced the effect I intended.

"Thank you. That would be fine." I settled far back in the banquette so I was unseen by the rest of the bar's habitues who had begun to mutter a little among themselves, obviously to gossip about me.

The lady who had befriended me went behind the bar, said something to the impassive barman. He shook his head and pointed to the rear door. I began to worry again. The woman said something else. He shrugged. She came back toward me.

"Looks like your father ducked out for a few minutes. Through the alley door."

"Oh, no!"

"Don't worry. If he said he'd meet you here, he'll be back." She smiled. "I like your father, the little I saw of him."

Most women would, I thought. But charm and integrity were not quite the same thing. I was beginning to be frightened for him. Something must have happened. The people he was afraid of . . . What had they done?

"Thank you," I said. "He sounded very positive on the phone. I know he wants very much to see me."

"Of course, he does. Anybody could tell that. Here comes your grasshopper."

The little glass topped by green foam arrived and I began to drink, trying to concentrate on the creme de menthe, the foam, anything to take up time. Dark Bruno's expressionless face broke into what I could only think was a kind of amused contempt. I felt more and more conspicuous.

How long was it since I had come in here? I glanced at my wrist, but I had taken off my watch before I left the hotel. I looked around the edge of the banquette. There was a clock, also psychedelically lighted, over the other end of the bar, but I couldn't make out the time.

I finished the grasshopper, tilting the glass to drink the last of the foam. The woman who seemed to run the place was standing before me. She looked surprisingly sympathetic.

"I think maybe he has changed his mind for tonight. He is sure to call you again tomorrow. Have you far to go? Live very far out?"

I got up. My knees were shaking. I stiffened them with an effort. "Not far, thank you. The Saint Francis. The next block."

She was surprised, and I noted with some ironic amusement that she couldn't help looking over my unprepossessing clothes. I paid for the drink, thanked her and walked out. I stood there on the sidewalk looking around. He was obviously nowhere on the street. I took a deep breath and walked around the corner to the alley. He had gone out here but it was clear to me that nothing beyond a pair of roving cats and a dozen ashcans inhabited the alley now.

I started walking back around the corner. A drunk shuffled up to me and mumbled something. I didn't wait to find out what it was. I walked rapidly up toward Geary Street and the hotel. In that block-long walk I saw no one who seemed the least likely to have threatened Father. When I reached the hotel, I looked back. The streets were momentarily deserted. Whatever had frightened Father away from our meeting was certainly not in evidence at this hour.

I went up to my room, but couldn't sleep. I kept listening for the telephone. Finally I did get to sleep, awaking late in the morning of a sunny day, piercingly sunny after the usual wind had scuttled the clouds away to the East and over the Sierras. I woke up with that peculiar dread hanging over me even before I opened my eyes. Something was wrong. Father was in trouble.

I reached for the telephone and called Adam McKendrick's office. I had only looked up one number, although there were two. The one number was busy. I felt around for the phone book, dragged it up and searched for Adam's name. I dialed the second number and this time heard the soft, but undoubtedly charming voice of Adam's secretary.

"Mr. McKendrick? No. I'm afraid he is out of

the office now. On an important matter. Adam has been very busy this morning. May I ask who is calling?"

Adam has been busy? Sounded very personal to me!

I gave my name and her voice changed noticeably. It was full of excitement. "But Miss Tracey, Mr. McKendrick was to have seen you this morning. Very important, he said. In fact, a matter of life and death. He was joking, of course. But—"

"Thank you. I understand. I'm sure he will be here any time now." I clicked off in a hurry and looked up the number at the museum exhibit on Fisherman's Wharf.

A crabbed male voice answered. Since it wasn't Leah Chandragar or her son, I guessed it must be Chato, he of the perennially cross disposition.

"Yeah. You want?"

"This is Barbara Tracey. Is my father there?"

"Nope."

That sounded definite. "May I speak to Mrs. Chandragar?"

"She's around payin' the bills. This place don't run on nothin', you know."

"Well then, her son. May I speak to Verne . . . Mr. Chandragar?"

"Him I can produce. You holding on?"

"Yes. I'm holding."

He left. I was so worried I began to tap rapidly on the phone. It seemed forever before I heard

Verne's pleasantly normal-voice in the background.

"Who? Me? Well, that's good news. My stock's looking up." He came on the line. "Hello, there. This Barbara? What are you doing today? I'm the best city guide you'll run across. Say the word."

I couldn't bring myself to laugh or treat his friendly offers with the light touch they needed.

"Verne, have you seen my father?"

He seemed a little surprised. "Seen Tom? Not today. No. What did he say when you saw him yesterday?"

"I didn't see him yesterday. He had been here apparently, but left before I got back." This brought on a complete silence. I said finally, "Are you still there?"

"I'm here. Where the hell did he go then?"

Didn't he know? I was under the impression that Father and Leah Chandragar lived together. Weren't they lovers? But, of course, there was no reason why a man Verne Chandragar's age must live at home. Maybe he just didn't know.

"Do you think your mother would know if he is home—that is, do you think she might have seen him?"

Verne seemed more lively. "I'll sure find out. What say we get together somewhere and take in —say, a ballgame? The Giants meet the Dodgers out at Candlestick."

"Thanks, but I'm a little worried. I'd really like

to see Father before I make any plans. Verne, I'd appreciate it if you could find out anything at all about him. You see, I had an appointment with him . . . he called me last night. But he didn't keep the appointment. He seemed terribly nervous, and then he didn't show up."

Verne was refreshingly unconcerned.

"Oh, well, Tom always was a kind of wanderer. I wouldn't worry too much. One time when he owed Mom a few thousand, he just up and vanished. Showed up later, with the money. We thought maybe he'd been dropped in the Bay or something. But he showed. And with the money. That's old Tom. He's just as likely to turn up in Alohaland. Or Hong Kong. Tom's like that. I wouldn't take this business seriously. On the level, Barb."

Barb? Well, who cared? Adam's secretary called him "Adam." The thing that really worried me was Father's panic last night. He was terrified of something, and only minutes after, he disappeared. Where was he now? Running away? Or had he been caught by those people he was so afraid of?

"If you could have heard his voice on the telephone . . ."

"Probably broke. He gambles a little. Maybe he's got some gambling crowd on his tail. . . . You won't go to the ballgame then? Hot dogs, cold beer, peanuts and popcorn. The works."

I made an effort and laughed. "Sounds wonderful. But not today. Maybe tomorrow."

"The Giants are on the road tomorrow." He sighed. "Oh, well, I'll give you a call anyway."

"Why not? And thank you, Verne. You're probably right about Father. Good-bye."

"If I hear anything from old Tom I'll let you know."

I thanked him again and hung up. I couldn't quite believe Father had gone away without even a word to Leah or her son, or to me. He hadn't gone away willingly. And he needed money. How was he getting along? If, of course, he was still alive.

I wanted to remain in my room in case anyone called about Father; so I ordered up a simple breakfast and went in to shower. I was still in the shower when someone knocked on the door and I called "Come in," supposing it was my breakfast. I was startled when I came into the sitting room in a too thin Pucci silk robe, to find myself under the interested eyes of Adam McKendrick. I grabbed at the skirt of my robe, testing the silk-covered buttons, but Adam's faint smile was more disturbing. It was neither lascivious nor amused. Just a little sad, a kind of rueful and gentle humor.

"Good morning, Barbara. I guess you didn't expect me. I'd like to say I'm sorry. Afraid I'd be a hypocrite."

I was polite, and then I couldn't resist his gentleness. I broke into a smile. "Thank you. I'm afraid I'm awfully late. But I was expecting my breakfast. I'd ask you to join me, only I'm sure you ate hours ago. You're the kind who does everything properly."

He crossed the room, took my hands, and before I guessed what he was doing, he kissed me. It was what I thought of suddenly as a "good morning, dear wife" kiss, and light as it was I suddenly reciprocated, touching his freshly shaved cheek with my lips. He was far more moved than I had expected him to be. The knowledge gave me a warm and wonderful confidence. I looked up at him flippantly.

"Don't you like a little of your own medicine?"

He looked at me a long minute before speaking. It was unnerving. When he did speak, there was that same gentleness which had troubled me the moment I saw him standing so unexpectedly in my sitting room.

"I love a little of my own medicine. Have you forgiven me for whatever made you so angry last night?"

I shrugged and withdrew my hands from his clasp.

"Don't be silly. I wasn't angry with you. I just had things to do. If you didn't come for breakfast, and you certainly haven't come for a date, it's got to be business; so start in while I dress . . ." I saw his smile flash again, and his eyebrows go up.

I added, "That is, if you stay here and wait for my breakfast to arrive. You can even drink some of the coffee."

"You aren't very generous. I really deserve at least a preview of my favorite client." But he did as he was told.

I went into the bedroom and dressed, talking to him as I did so.

"Why did you come? Still protecting me against imaginary dangers? You should have been out protecting my poor father."

"What do you mean by that?" His voice was louder, obviously near the open doorway.

"Never mind. I'll tell you when I come out."

His voice suddenly lost the likable, teasing note. "That is what I want to talk to you about. Your father. It seems there was a bad mistake made. Or we think so, at any rate. The set of fingerprints . . . Well, let's say there's been some clever work done by your friend Tom Tracey."

"My friend Tom Tracey! What do you mean? What has Father done?" I came to the doorway, still zipping my dress. I was so anxious about this obviously bad news of Father that I made no objection when he came to my rescue and finished zipping me. He moved me around to face him, but so gently I felt there was more to this than a simple flirtation or even a perfectly sincere love affair. When he didn't speak, I thought to forestall him by saying quickly, "Father was in danger last night; so you needn't tell me about what a—a villain he is. You'd do better to look for the man, or men, who threatened him last night."

He lowered his hands to my shoulders. His eyes had always had a powerful effect upon me, but their warm, compassionate gaze at this moment only worried me.

"Please," I whispered, hardly able to control my voice or my emotions, "if you have something to tell me, and I'm sure it's bad, tell me straight out."

He took a deep breath. "We've found . . . we think we have found Tom Tracey."

"He's dead!"

"No! Nothing like that. At least, we can't be sure. I've no idea what happened to your Tom Tracey. Look—I'm not getting through this thing. Darling, we all supposed the set of fingerprints belonged to your Tom Tracey. When your Chicago company and I checked this Tracey there seemed to be no loopholes. We'd received the fingerprints, photos . . . unmistakably the Tom Tracey who was your father."

I removed those protective hands of his and sat down slowly.

"Are you trying to tell me I don't know my own father?"

"I'm afraid . . . the truth is, I'm not sure."

CHAPTER 8

I was torn between fury at this hideous "mistake" and the lingering worry over the fate of the man I knew as Tom Tracey. I pretended to ignore his fumbling on about this new father he'd obviously dug up. Even he wasn't sure.

"Never mind that. What has happened to my own Tom Tracey? He was in danger. I know that."

Adam was quite surprised that I didn't ask about the new "father" he had located. "I don't know. He's probably run away. He must have heard about the other Tracey."

So cowardice was to be added to the rest of my father's unsavory traits!

I said with a flippancy that even shook me, "I'll bet my Tracey could lick your Tracey!"

"Darling . . . Barbara . . ."

"Don't! And above all, don't tell me how sorry you are about all this." I hated him for that sympathy in his voice and his manner. It was he who made me believe in Tom Tracey in the first place, and now he was trying to take away the image, the warm and comfortable relationship he had helped me to find with my Tom Tracey.

I suppose even patient men have their limits. He stepped back, his features stiffening to cool and very businesslike good manners.

"You are right, of course. It was entirely our fault. Glenn Rivercombe wanted to call you as soon as he learned of the—masquerade, or whatever it was. I asked him not to call until I explained it all to you. I've made a botch of it; so I might as well let Rivercombe handle it from here on."

Things were getting out of hand. He started to the door and the phone buzzed. He was passing the telephone and I couldn't help being relieved when he stopped and waited.

"That may be Rivercombe now."

"Yes," I said and reached for the phone. Adam was moving on now. I put my hand over the mouthpiece of the phone. "Don't go. He will probably want to talk to you." I said "Hello" to the caller, and Verne Chandragar's voice greeted me.

"Hi! Verne the sleuth here. Good news."

"Oh, Verne! How wonderful! Have you located him?"

Adam opened the outside door with a very loud and grating noise. Then he acted as if he had overcome some strong, angry determination to stalk out without another word. He said, "If you want to see your father . . . the—the other Tracey, someone else from my office can meet you later today and take you to him."

"Take me to him?" Someone else would take me to him.

"What's that?" Verne cut in on the phone. "You talking to me, Barb?"

"No, not you, Verne. Adam . . . what is wrong with him, this fellow who calls himself Tom Tracey?"

"Later. When you aren't so busy with your social activities," Adam announced in the clipped manner that reminded me very forcibly of the maddening private eye I had first known. He went out, slamming the door.

"What's going on up there?" Verne wanted to know. "Sounds like the walls are caving in."

"No. Just a man in a temper. Tell me about Father. Where did you find him? What really happened last night?"

Verne said lightly, "Like I said, he owes these

Vegas jokers a packet; so, when he couldn't get you last night, right away, he got hold of Mom. She looks tough, but she's a soft touch if you handle her right. So he took off. He'll be back in town, soon as he gets this business worked out and the heat's off."

"You mean he just took off, like that, without a word to me, after all the worry he put me through last night?" I was terribly hurt, and yet I knew I had no right to be. Father had his own life, and until a few days ago it had nothing to do with me. But it didn't help when Verne reminded me of it.

"Well, honey—Barb, I mean, we've had the old boy quite a while longer than you. It's only natural he'd turn to Mother when he's in trouble. He always does. You still busy today? How about that ballgame?"

I hesitated. I wasn't crazy about baseball, but then, I wasn't crazy about sitting around the hotel all day wondering about that other Tom Tracey, either.

"Why not? What time shall I be ready?"

As it turned out, the baseball game raised my spirits considerably. For one thing, Verne was a passionate Giants rooter, and the Giants lost. Ordinarily, this would have made for a pretty gloomy date, but Verne behaved with such mixtures of wild elation and despair that he kept me laughing hysterically. He allowed me to pay for the beer and the hot dogs—he ate three—but he bought the popcorn. All the way into town on the bus he replayed the game, to the advantage of the Giants, with the help of the other pro-Giant passengers.

When we walked to my hotel from the bus stop, I asked him, "What did Father say about leaving all his friends so abruptly? Did he tell you about why he didn't call me again after letting me wait all that time? I could have helped him, financially, if no other way."

Verne stopped in the middle of what I suspected was a mental replaying of the game. He looked a trifle confused.

"Well, the fact is, I didn't talk to him."

"You didn't! But I thought—"

"Mom's the one. He came to her like he often does, got a little drink money, bus money, or whatever, and just took off. But don't worry. He's pulled this a lot. It's nothing new with your father. He's probably up in Reno right now, recouping his losses at the crap tables."

I took a breath, glanced at him and saw that I now had his attention.

"Suppose—just suppose—he isn't my father."

He stopped abruptly again. A smartly dressed woman shopper walking rapidly behind him just missed piling into us.

"You're putting me on!"

I said, "I wish to God I was."

We didn't say any more until we had crossed the street and he looked up at the noble old gray facade of the hotel and asked me, "You going to leave it like that? You mean there's something wrong about Tom?"

"I don't know. I wish I did."

He leaned against the showcase window near a side entrance of the hotel and shook his head.

"I can't figure it. He often does this. I mean like last night. Bums it from Mom and powders off. Has he done something to turn you off?"

I asked levelly, without any of the doubts and suspicions and pain I felt, "Do you know any reason why I should be turned off Tom Tracey?"

"Nothing. So help me! I'd have sworn the guy was on the level. He and Mom talked about you until it nearly came out of my ears. It just doesn't seem possible he isn't leveling with us." He looked at me hard. Those dark eyes could be very hard, I discovered. "Or have you some real bad stuff on him? Something we don't know."

I couldn't answer him. I had no idea where the truth was. I told Verne that I hadn't any idea whether there had been a trick, or that our Tom Tracey might be a fraud.

"I may know more after tonight."

He looked interested. "Tonight? What happens tonight?"

I had no idea at that moment why I didn't continue to be honest. "Well, no matter where he is, Father ought to call me, especially to apologize for raising so much trouble last night. Or even to get money." I watched him without seeming to. But he appeared only reasonably interested.

"Well, he might just do that. Look, I hope you had a good time today. I really mean that, Barb."

I told him I had a great time and that he'd taken my mind off a lot of problems.

"Yeah. Three or four million. Bye for now."

I laughed, but as I left him I found his remark less and less funny. Also, the euphoria of our silly, happy afternoon was wearing off. As I walked the length of the lobby, I turned around several times, but saw no one familiar, nothing to explain the sense I had of being watched.

In the spacious hall upstairs, enchantingly "dated" with its Regency wallpaper of black on gold, I saw a tall shadow in the cross-hall leading to my suite. I didn't dare to hope it was Adam McKendrick, who had changed his mind about taking me to see his new version of Tom Tracey. Wondering who it might be, I hesitated. But he stepped into the main hall and with great relief I saw that the vaguely sinister shadow actually was Adam. He gave me no friendly opening. Obviously, he still remembered and was angered by our morning quarrel.

"Enjoy your date?" he asked coldly.

"Enormously. Have you been waiting long?"

"Oh, no. Just got here. My secretary couldn't make it. She had a—dental appointment."

"I'm so sorry. What a shame! But now that you are here, I suppose that's nearly as good."

He gave me a look that was half nasty, half amused, and then asked me, "Did this Chandragar tell you anything about the fellow involved with his mother?"

"My Tom Tracey, you mean."

"That one. Yes."

I said stiffly, "Father was in a little difficulty. He went out of town on a business deal. He'll be back in a few days. I know Father when it comes to that sort of thing."

"I hope so. We've quite a little business with him ourselves." His grimness about my Tom Tracey shook me.

Realizing the serious mess Father had gotten himself into, I tried hard to make this stubborn man see it. "Adam, don't you understand? My Tom Tracey is everything I ever imagined my father to be. He's a kind of dream come true. I don't mind his—well, his roguishness, his peccadilloes, because he's all the bright, delightful things I remember from the old days. Now you're going to tell me he is a crook, or a cheat, or something or other. But I just don't care!"

I thought his expression softened a little, but it was hard to tell. He took my arm.

"Come along. Have you any idea how late it is?"

"Come along where? What is this? I can't run out without a jacket or something. You know these foggy evenings."

At least, I had my way in this. He came back to my sitting room while I got an Edwardian velvet jacket and he stuck each of my arms into the sleeves as if he were dressing a child. I found myself surprisingly happy, and made no stupid objections. He put on the finishing touches by turning up my collar and for an instant, as his hands lingered on my throat and I looked up at him, we had that cord of communion which we had experienced briefly, but delightfully, once or twice before.

We remained in this close, intimate situation for several seconds before mutually realizing its embarrassment in our present state of suspended hostilities.

"Well," he said finally, removing his hands as if my neck had burned him, "this isn't getting to our appointment."

Not to be outdone, I agreed with enormous enthusiasm, "Righto! Let's go. We're killing time!"

It was not until we were in Adam's car and driving to some unpleasant place, I didn't know where, to see a man I didn't want to see, that I understood I was doing something I had no desire to do.

"Where are we going?" I asked sullenly as we headed out through the Stockton Street tunnel. "Not that I care, frankly."

"I'm flattered."

I looked at him. "Why?"

"You don't care where you are going; so I can only assume you are in this car because you like the company."

I had to laugh at that. "Now you've guessed my ugly little secret."

"Ugly secret! That goes for me!"

We felt better after that and as we drove through the edges of Chinatown and on toward the Italian section called North Beach, we exchanged small talk. I still didn't know where we were going, but I knew evening had come on, and the world had that night look, half infernal regions and half twinkling golden lights, like the way to an *Arabian Nights* treasure.

Adam pointed to our right, toward a long, feeble series of lights. "Remember hearing about The Barbary Coast?"

"Before the Earthquake?" I sat up and looked off in that direction.

"Before the Fire," he corrected me like a loyal

native son. "Well, that used to be the heart of the old Barbary Coast. Reasonably respectable now. That's Pacific Street. Nicknamed in the old days: *Terrific Street*."

"Sounds marvelous."

"It wasn't," he said. "Not if you were being shanghaied. My grandfather was shanghaied on that street."

This made it much more fascinating, and of course, my heart was wrung for a young man looking exactly like Adam (in my mind's eye) being slipped a "mickey" and loaded on a deep-water sailing vessel in the harbor.

We crossed Columbus Avenue. We were in the middle of the busy Italian district. Women were still shopping in some of the little local stores, where I suddenly knew there were great jars of long, unbroken spaghetti, and where dozens of strong-smelling but succulent sausages hung above the wooden counter.

"I wonder how I know that," I murmured, more or less to myself.

Adam glanced at me. "Know what?"

"I had the funniest feeling . . . as if I'd been in one of those grocery stores before."

"Maybe you were."

"No. We lived on Nob Hill. The unfashionable side. Nowhere around here." I leaned out the window and stared at the narrow buildings, mostly two-story, often built over garages, or over those fascinating little corner groceries. I had the distinct feeling the French call *deja vu.* I seemed to have been here before.

Adam read my confusion and reached over with his free hand in that wonderfully comforting way of his that I had noticed, and enjoyed, the previous night. He closed his hand over my slightly nervous fingers.

"Maybe you've seen pictures. God knows there are enough books about San Francisco, and full of pictures. You're sure of having looked them over, at least."

My agreement was slow, but I was inclined to agree with him, or at any rate, I was hopeful of accepting that explanation eventually.

After climbing the lower reaches of another hill, we turned abruptly and parked before a pink stucco house over its own garage. I stared at the facade as we started up the steps.

"It should be white. With red trim." It was a weird feeling to hear myself say something that seemed to be dredged up from my subconscious.

Adam looked at me. "Why?"

I had a feeling I was being pumped and I didn't like it. "Because that's more artistically satisfying. To me, anyway." I added with sly innocence, "What did you think I had in mind?"

"Then you haven't seen this house before?"

"I don't think so. Who lives here?" I was being quite sincere about this, although I was certain he wanted to tell me it was owned, or maybe rented by his version of my father.

"Family with an Italian name. It doesn't come back to you?"

"Caruso? Alioto? Christopher Columbus?"

"Very funny. Ah! Here we are." The door was opening. I could hear my own heartbeat. I knew that in spite of all my determination to stand by my own Tom Tracey, I half expected to see a man looking like his twin appear in the doorway. Instead, I found myself looking at a middle-aged woman with neat, greying dark hair and brown eyes whose direct, yet not unsympathetic gaze seemed oddly familiar to me.

"Good evening, Mr. McKendrick. I see you were able to bring Barbara-Jane. We weren't sure, when you were delayed, that she would come. She always did have a mind of her own."

Adam shook hands with her. "Yes. The truth is, I think she was curious about this. Barbara, this is Mrs. Alfredo Cortapassi."

Lost in a maze of memories that made little sense and seemed to have occurred in another lifetime, I murmured slowly, "Rose Cortapassi. You had black hair and you used to wear a tiny miniature rose in your hair. And you smelled wonderfully of roses and lovely things."

"The rose in the hair, it was a common custom in the late Forties. And Alfredo liked it. But thank you. You have not changed. Here is my husband. This is little Barbara-Jane, *caro mio!*"

A stout man whose dignity was belied by his twinkling eyes had stepped into the doorway behind her. He startled me, though not unpleasantly, by reaching out, pulling me to him in the hall that smelled of savory spaghetti sauce, and kissed me on both cheeks.

"Of course, I remember Thomas' little one! I would have known her anywhere."

"What a liar he is!" his wife exclaimed with a brusque fondness I liked. "But come in. Both of you. Imagine saying you had not changed from the child of three to the beautiful young lady of—"

"Twenty-five."

Mr. Cortapassi boomed, "What nonsense you talk! As if you could be twenty-five? It is like yesterday. Through this hall. Parlor on the left and dining room beyond. But you will remember, Little Barbara-Jane."

I caught Adam's grin at this description of a woman five feet-six inches tall, and then we all laughed, including Mrs. Cortapassi. The truth is, however, I remembered little items about their house. A huge red album on a stand between two overstuffed chairs. The genuine old glass Tiffany lamp on the mantel above a fake fireplace with an electric heater. The built-in bookcases and the arch that together separated the parlor from the dining room. And almost more than anything else, the dozen herbs and the tomato paste and the mushrooms and endless items that went into the spaghetti sauce Mr. Cortapassi used to spend a whole day preparing.

I turned around very slowly. I knew they were all watching me. I felt they were analyzing my every breath, every move, but in the case of the Cortapassis, their interest seemed friendly, warm. Adam's interest was more intense and anxious, and it worried me. Were they all planning a surprise for me? A shock?

I tried not to let them know how nervous I was. I said gaily, "I'm trying to think of something else. A dark, cozy room with a leather bed. A room that smelled faintly of an old-fashioned scent. Attar of Roses, maybe. And yet—pipe smoke, too."

Rose Cortapassi laughed. "The Attar of Roses was there to drown the remains of Alfredo's pipe smoke. Alfredo's study across the hall."

"My study at night. Her sewing room in the daytime." Mr. Cortapassi explained to Adam, "Thomas used to put little Barbara-Jane to sleep in there on my old leather sofa. Not that they stayed late. Thomas was careful about it. Afraid of that icy female he was married—"

"Alfredo!"

"Sorry." He shrugged his big shoulders. "But in this house, truth is important."

I had felt a quick twinge of resentment on Mother's behalf, but even the resentment was hypocritical. I remembered suddenly how Father had begged Mother to join us in visiting his old friends, and how cutting she was, imitating Mr. Cortapassi's slight girth that gave him an amusing walk, or Rose's "Arrogance, Tom! Arrogance in that ridiculous woman." Yes. Mr. Cortapassi was right about Mother. But it hurt, all the same.

We went across the hall and into the sewing-room-study. Mr. Cortapassi was his exuberant self.

"Behold your old hiding place, Miss Barbara-Jane! Remember the big bear who used to ride you around the room on his back, and down that hall? You really kicked this old bear good and hard to make him go. And—" He moved away from the end of the old leather couch. His eyes were gleaming with excitement and tears. "Remember this old fellow? You called him Father, but we called him our dear friend . . . Thomas."

The old man on the couch sat up. His hair, once red, was kinky and white. The freckles had become an occasional liver spot on the face and hands. He was thinner. His grin was pitifully shy, a hopeful attempt at a smile. But it was the only young and familiar thing about him.

CHAPTER 9

"Hello," I said when it seemed that he wasn't going to be able to get the words out. *Whatever words they were.*

"Barb—Barbara, honey. You look so different."

I was furious at the pity I felt welling up in me. I managed to express the resentment rather than the sadness and pity. "I should look different, shouldn't I? After twenty years."

Someone stirred nervously behind me. They all probably thought I was cruel for acting this way to someone they considered my father. As for me, I didn't know what to think and, unfortunately for me, my own deep-rooted emotional feelings told me there was just a chance this was my real father. A father far from the romantic adventurer and charmer I had always imagined him to be.

He sat up with a little difficulty and Alfredo Cortapassi bustled over to help him. Everything seemed to anger me, even that good-hearted, kindly effort of a friend. *They are trying to play on my sympathy,* I told myself. *But I won't fall for it.*

I did, though, as might be expected, but I didn't let it show immediately.

"Are you sick? What seems to be wrong?"

Thomas Tracey grinned. He looked hauntily like a shadowed, older version of my own Tom Tracey.

"Arthritis of the spine. I'm not always flat on my back like this. It comes and goes. I can walk. It's just that sometimes it's a little more painful than other times. Started years ago after a loading accident on the docks. I'm really not quite the half-man I seem . . . Honey."

There was a definite hesitation before that endearment. Had he been coached, and was he unsure of himself, or simply unsure of me?

I said, "I'm sorry. I know it can be very painful. Mr. Rivercombe has trouble with bursitis." It was so awkward! Except for brief, meaningless expressions of sympathy, there was no conversation I could conduct with him. It was nothing like my instant rapport with my Tom Tracey. And the presence of three very interested witnesses didn't make it any better, either.

Mrs. Cortapassi seemed to understand this. She said to her husband, "I think the water for the spaghetti is boiling over. Come!"

Alfredo Cortapassi lingered, reluctant to take the hint. "No . . . not yet. I do not smell anything burning. Besides, it is very moving to see a father and daughter united in this beautiful way. This is a happy time." With great force he blew his nose into a huge handkerchief.

"Alfredo!" said his wife and left the room.

"Coming, dearest one," he called hastily, and vanished after her.

In other circumstances I would have found this little domestic scene highly amusing. But along with everything else, I resented Adam's forcing me into this fake relationship with a man for whom I felt absolutely nothing but pity.

The man calling himself Thomas Tracey made what appeared to be a valiant effort to sit up straight and make room for me. I didn't want to sit down next to him, poor man! He was trying so hard to be fatherly, and except for the general contours of his face and the occasional timbre of his voice, I still felt him to be completely foreign to me. But Adam was watching and I felt like such a heel that I did sit down in an embarrassingly hesitant way, practically on the edge of the couch, and then made rapid conversation to keep him from touching me.

"When I'm here, I keep thinking of the cats we used to try and adopt. Remember how we found that wonderful stray, all gold with little stripes? What was his name? Something silly, but just right for him." I glanced at the old man beside me. "What was that darned name?"

I waited, my fingers cold, my heartbeat increased.

He looked up at Adam, who was frowning. Then he glanced at me, furtively, I thought.

"I'm afraid I don't quite . . . remember. Seems to me, your mother never allowed animals in the flat."

That was true enough. He had been well schooled. I stared up at Adam but he refused to look guilty. I was the one who tried to trick this poor man. Instead of owning up, I persisted in maintaining that we had tried to bring in cats, and that there really was a gold, striped Tabby. Actually, there had been one, but it belonged to the neighbors in the first-floor flat. This Thomas Tracey obviously didn't remember that. If he had ever known it!

We talked about other things, pointless rambling. Neither Thomas Tracey nor Adam had enough nerve to bring up proofs of the man's past, and when Alfredo Cortapassi came in to call us to supper, we had not really gotten anywhere and I, for one, was terribly relieved at the interruption.

We went to wash up. The house was warmly old-fashioned, with one bathroom. They showed me in first. The towels and soaps and bath perfume were all modern, but the location of the room itself and the placement of the window seemed familiar. I remembered how high the window had seemed when I was three years old. And I remembered once when a celebration was going on, with fireworks in the streets below us—I think it was Columbus Day—I climbed up on the toilet seat and tried to peer out at the night sky. Instead of seeing fireworks, I had slipped and hit my chin on the windowsill. I still carried the scar.

Yes. I admitted it to myself finally. I had been here before, long ago, with Father. The point remained, however: was this bedraggled and sick creature the real Thomas Tracey? If he wasn't, then Rose and Alfredo Cortapassi must be cheats and frauds, and I couldn't believe that. Besides, I vaguely remembered them.

I came out of the bathroom and walked into the kitchen.

"Do you remember the dessert we used to have?" Rose asked me as she bustled around in her big, pleasant, Mother Hubbard apron.

I thought back. "I do! It seems to me everyone gave me a spoonful of spumoni when I'd finished my own. I'm afraid I made an awful pig of myself."

"Not at all. You were a very thin child. Much too thin, Alfredo and I always thought. We tried to fatten you up."

She had dropped the long spaghetti into the boiling water and we looked at each other for a minute, recovering some of the warm, dear relationship we had once known. I turned and hugged her. Very gradually, hesitantly, her arms went around me. There was the faint suggestion of tears in her eyes before she blinked and said in a businesslike way, "Go in the dining room and see if you remember where you used to sit."

I pushed open the door and walked around the long, heavy, old-fashioned table with its snowy cloth. The cloth was thick double damask. There were more glasses shimmering on the table than I was used to seeing when I was invited to dinner in the middle-class homes of my friends and fellow workers at the Rivercombe offices. No coffee cups and saucers here, but two wine glasses at each place, plus water glasses already filled. And no ice in the glasses. Everything pointed to delicious, old-fashioned family meals. In the welter of linen or plastic place mats and endless coffee that accented today's modern dinners, I had almost forgotten these touches of another, and in some ways, better day.

I walked around the table, mentally placing myself where I seemed to have been most at home many years ago. I pictured myself in each chair, and thought of the windows, and the view, and the sight I had of every detail in those days. But nothing seemed natural until I remembered the table's edge, the way I had pleated the lovely tablecloth because it was the closest thing I could reach while the adults talked long and—to me—boringly around the dessert plates.

I almost shouted: "I remember!"

Mrs. Cortapassi came in through the swinging door. She looked happier, her splendid features softened by her smile.

"You remember which chair you sat in?"

"Better! I remember you put two sofa cushions under me to raise me up. The top cushion had a cover made of different bits of material. They weren't all the same weight and I could feel against my bare legs the velvet and the satin pieces, and then a rougher material. Wool?"

"My old piecework cushion." She went into the living room to the couch under the wide front window. "This one?"

It was old and faded and shabby, but it was the cushion I remembered, and I liked it better for its shabbiness. I examined it and set it back on the couch. The once bright pieces of material were sewn together with a kind of cross-stitch and some of the stitches had broken during the years. They were repaired with different colored thread, all of which gave the pillow the look of a kaleidoscope of delicate colors.

"I love it," I said quite honestly. "It makes everything seem warm and cozy."

She smiled and called the men in to dinner. No one had drunk cocktails. As Mr. Cortapassi said now in his booming voice, "Better for the taste buds. They are dulled when liquor is drunk before dinner." Thomas Tracey grinned wanly as he moved to the table on Adam's arm.

"In thirty years it is my only disagreement with my old friend," Tracey said.

I tried to help him into the high-backed chair my father had taken in the old days, but Adam was there and I only got in the way. My chair was set in its old, familiar place between Alfredo, at the head, and Rosa at the foot of the table where she was handy to the kitchen. I did not feel at ease under that double scrutiny: Thomas looking expectant, hopeful, and Adam, puzzled, still thoughtful. And disapproving of me, I was sure. I told myself he probably thought I had a great deal of my mother's chilly character, and was unsympathetic. The truth is, I am not usually so cold-hearted, but I had this terrible, gnawing suspicion coupled with keen disappointment when I compared this faded Thomas Tracey with the strong and dominating Tom Tracey who so closely coincided with my mental picture of my father.

"Not quite like the old days, eh?" asked Mr. Cortapassi after the partitioned plates of antipasto had been rapidly emptied. He took all our dishes in front of his place and filled them with the spaghetti, using both hands as always, then crowned the pasta with succulent, mouthwatering sauce, and finally framed this dish with lovingly created meatballs.

We were all too intent on watching his every move to concentrate on his remark, but as we received our plates, and the fresh-grated cheese was passed around, I insisted sincerely, "But it's exactly the same, except for Adam being here, of course. Just as wonderful as ever."

"No pillows needed for Barbara-Jane," Mr. Cortapassi shouted in triumph, and after we laughed and agreed, we were silent, devoting ourselves to the important task at hand.

"You find San Francisco changed very much?" Mrs. Cortapassi asked me as she returned from the kitchen, opening and closing the door with a deft swing of her hips. She set the pieces of hot sour French bread on the table and very soon that disappeared too.

I said when I could get a breath between bites, "I love some of the new things. More trees downtown. And Ghirardelli Square and the Cannery.

But I hate the skyscrapers with those horrible glass bugs that crawl up and down the outside of buildings."

"Glass bugs!" asked Alfredo, greatly astonished.

Adam explained about the elevators and "Tracey" nodded.

"They give your stomach a nasty ride. No getting around it."

I stopped eating, but only for a few seconds. *My* father has never minded heights. He told me once that one of his first jobs was painting gilt on the tip of the flag pole over the YMCA building.

"I hate elevators nowadays anyway," I said, using the same gimmick I had used with the first Tom Tracey.

Mr. and Mrs. Cortapassi looked at me with interest. I wondered if I should reveal the story of the Madrid accident, but a glance at the Thomas Tracey who sat across the table kept me silent. He was speaking, explaining to the Cortapassis something he couldn't possibly know.

"Barbara-Jane had a critical accident in an elevator in Europe. Shook her up pretty bad. Can't blame her."

"No, surely not," Mrs. Cortapassi agreed. "I was in a department store years ago when an elevator stopped between floors. It was a long time before I could get over that feeling of being closed in. . . . Will you all have spumoni?"

We groaned and protested but no one flatly refused. I helped her clear the table and when I returned Adam and Alfredo Cortapassi were discussing the political situation in a local mayoralty race. Thomas Tracey sat there looking a little out of things.

I stopped beside him, and asked awkwardly, "How are you getting along these days?" I couldn't bring myself to add the hypocritical "Father."

He made an effort to smile. "I live on my compensation. Not bad at all. Al and I made up a right nice little place behind the garage recently. Plenty of light, and there's heat. We play a lot of checkers. He beats me raw, but I've got him licked at rummy."

I felt selfish and cheap and as insensitive as Mother. It would be so easy to see that this man was lavishly provided for. And I meant to do just that if he was some kind of more-or-less innocent dupe, but I couldn't help feeling I was being maneuvered into this and I deeply resented it. I felt like a recalcitrant child being dragged along kicking and screaming to something I didn't want to face.

I went back to get plates of spumoni and set them out while Mrs. Cortapassi brought in the coffee cups and the electric percolator. While we were all thawing the ice cream with the hot coffee, I asked suddenly, "How did you know about my accident in the Madrid elevator?"

Everyone stopped eating. They all knew I was addressing Thomas Tracey, but I could see that my question involved them as well. Spoons dropped audibly onto china.

Thomas Tracey, however seemed more puzzled than alert.

"Your young friend Mr. McKendrick here told me after the mess about the fingerprints came out. The Union had a series and somehow, somebody got them mixed up. Finally, I guess one of the boys told Mr. McKendrick about me, and my prints matched, and that was all there was to it. He told me all about my little girl."

Adam neither agreed nor disagreed. I wondered what he was thinking. He certainly came to Tracey's rescue, whether intentionally or not.

"From what I hear, you're liable to have some skyscrapers above you here on the Hill."

Mrs. Cortapassi said sharply, "We vote against it. We march against it. Nothing works. We get them when we do not want them. It is the way everywhere. The individual is lost."

"My dearest one always votes against the incumbent," Alfredo told us and we laughed with him. Rose laughed too, but insisted, "I keep City Hall on its toes!"

When this memorable dinner was over and Mrs. Cortapassi and I did the dishes, I asked her, "How did you meet him again? I know we had to stop coming to see you before I was four years old."

"The purest accident. About six months ago, Alfredo went to some sort of union affair. Mr. Bridges was appearing, and some organizers from Hawaii. All the old-timers were there. Alfredo was late and he arrived just as Thomas was leaving. They bumped into each other. It was fate. Thomas recognized Alfredo instantly."

"I must do something to help him," I promised.

"Your father deserves a little help, I think. As I understand it, he was not responsible for the original separation and divorce."

I couldn't go quite that far. "Well, he did lie a great deal about his jobs. I don't know how many times Father told Mother he had a job when he didn't. But he was such a charmer. So—likable."

She admitted a little sadly, "It is true he has changed, grown older, not such a charmer, perhaps."

I must have startled her when I disagreed.

"I don't think so. I think my father is just as delightful and gallant and charming as ever."

"But—" She let that go, but she was troubled. I don't think she understood my reference to my own Tom Tracey.

Shortly after Adam and I said good night, thanking the Cortapassis with hugs (on my part) and enormous enthusiasm for the good time they had given us. Thomas Tracey hugged me shyly, embarrassed as if he expected to be rebuffed. I couldn't help it. I did my best. I suppose I wasn't a very good actress.

On the way back to my hotel Adam asked me if I would like a nightcap.

"Top of the Mark?" He glanced at me, smiled and added, "Inside elevator," but I made a face and said, "I'm full to the brim. Not tonight, thanks. Can I have a raincheck?"

"Any time. You know that."

We were silent. Then I asked, "Did you really tell him?"

"Tell who what?"

"You know. Did you tell that fellow about my fall in the elevator in Madrid?"

I thought for a breathless minute that he was going to say "yes" and if he did, I could never trust him again; for he couldn't possibly know about that Madrid business legitimately. I hadn't told him, and he could only know because he had spied on me in Europe for some far-reaching plan, such as the substitution of the fake Tracey.

"No. I didn't know."

"Then your precious Thomas Tracey lied."

"It would seem so," he admitted.

We talked about other things, and when he left me, we kissed good night, but we were both troubled and both suspicious. Though not, I hoped, of each other.

CHAPTER 10

There were so many ways I could have tricked Thomas Tracey into revealing himself, I was sure. But it would only be one more cruelty in a life that seemed, from the looks of him, one long failure. From Adam's attitude I guessed that he, too, was doing some re-thinking. Had he really covered the past of this fellow, Thomas Tracey? And how had the lives of this man and my Tom Tracey run parallel? They looked alike. But that could be purely coincidental.

Most curious of all: why had both claimants mentioned my Madrid experience with the elevator when no one should have known about it? Even Adam shouldn't have known. I had kept it a secret because, when it happened, I was sure its knowledge would keep my mother and her advisers from letting me go back to Europe on my own. But had I told anyone?

In spite of refusing Adam's nightcap invitation, I now felt far too nervous to go up to bed immediately. I rang for the elevator, then abruptly changed my mind and walked a few steps to the nearest bar, a quiet, subdued place at this hour, with the barman talking in low tones with two men at the far end of the bar. Nearer, a man and woman were drinking what appeared to be brandy and saying very little, but they were holding hands. My perverse imagination pictured them as "brief encounter" lovers, both married but not to each other, and carrying on a shabby but, of course, romantic affair.

I sat down at a small table near the entrance to the cafe, and when the barman came to get my order I took out a little notebook, with its gold pencil, and made notations in order to have something to do. No one paid any attention to me, however, although several times a shadow passed the open doorway, and every time I looked up, whoever seemed to be picketing the place was gone. A little later I sipped my Alfonse and did some thinking. I made lists of questions with which to trap either my Tom Tracey or the man I had met tonight. But the questions were useless. The old "Tom Tracey" was frail and sick. I couldn't completely cross him off. Even if he was a crook, a fake, I knew I would pay off the poor devil before we ended this charade.

"My father is Tom Tracey!"

The barman looked over at me.

"You say something, Miss?"

Embarrassed, I shook my head, took another sip and scribbled another question. But it was no use. I wasn't built for playing detective, trapping people. Besides, I might trap my own father! Just because that poor old man living with the Cortapassis had known something he shouldn't know, did that make him a stranger? Even if he was a crook, he could still be my father. In fact, from my knowledge of Father in the old days . . .

But I didn't pursue that further.

So now I had two fathers, both of whom were very likely liars and crooks, but on the other hand, this quality should make them much better cast in the role of my real father. I was just finishing my drink when a young woman suddenly appeared from nowhere to stand in front of me.

"Miss Tracey?"

I looked up. I guessed she was a hotel employee but it seemed extraordinary that she would know me well enough to ferret me out here and at this hour.

"There are a number of long-distance telephone messages that came in this evening, Miss Tracey. They seemed awfully urgent. Sorry."

I thanked her and took the neatly written slips

of paper. The top two were from Verne Chandragar and his mother, Leah Chandragar.

"You will find a light in your suite, Miss Tracey, about the messages. You can ignore that now. But there were so many calls, especially long distance, that when I saw you a few minutes ago, I thought . . ."

"Did you pass that doorway a few minutes ago?"

"No. I just came from the desk."

"You're very kind. Thank you so much. It's lucky you saw me. It's so late I mightn't have noticed the light or whatever, and just gone to bed." I had my fingers inside my handbag and found a bill. I slipped it into her hand in place of the sheaf of messages and we were both satisfied.

When she had gone, I looked through the slips. Three were from Mr. Rivercombe in Chicago, and one was from a "Mr. Thomas Michaels" of Reno, Nevada. I was puzzled, but only momentarily . . . Father. That is to say, *my* Tom Tracey, was up to his old tricks. Verne had thought Tom went up to Reno to make some money. Mister Thomas Michaels was merely my Tom Michael Tracey. Unfortunately, he hadn't left a phone number where he could be reached in Reno. But maybe that was why the Chandragars had called, to give me the information.

In my sitting room I called the museum exhibit while I shook off my jacket and stepped out of my shoes. There was no immediate answer. When the surly voice came on, I knew I would get little help there.

"Chato? Is it you?"

"Yeah. You're too late."

"Really? Too late for what?"

"They've all gone home. We're closing up."

Not surprising. It was after midnight. "I see. I'm sorry. Verne and Mrs. Chandragar both called me. It was about my—about Tom Tracey."

"He's gone."

"I know that!" I shouted. I was getting pretty sick of his eternal bad temper. "He has gone to Reno, Verne thinks."

He sounded slightly mollified by my unexpected bark. Or maybe, by some chance, I had scared him.

"They're after him. He owes some money. He better make it at craps or he's good as out. Them boys mean business."

"Do you know where he is staying?"

He laughed. It was a dry, unhumorous laugh that frightened me. "If I's to tell you that, I'd tell anybody. And your precious da-da wouldn't be floating his crap game very long. Not alive, anyways."

"Of course. I realize that. I'll call—what is Mrs. Chandragar's number?"

"She don't know where he is."

But I finally chiseled her number out of him, and

called. There was no answer. I looked up Verne's name in the phone book. I failed to find it. It was certainly too late to call Mr. Rivercombe at two-twenty A.M. Chicago time; so I gave up and went to bed.

I needn't have worried. Rivercombe's telegram arrived the next morning.

"BARBARA DEAR,

REGRET FINGERPRINT MIXUP. WRONG SET OBTAINED THROUGH CONFUSION ON NAMES. MCKENDRICK WILL HAVE EXPLAINED. BELIEVE ME SINCERELY SORRY. BUT YOU ARE PROBABLY REUNITED WITH REAL THOMAS TRACEY BY NOW. TRIED PHONING YOU TODAY AND TONIGHT. IMPOSTER WILL NOT ANNOY YOU FURTHER. PROSECUTION IN PROCESS.

AGAIN REGRETS,
GLENN RIVERCOMBE"

He told me nothing I hadn't known before. It was a remarkably stupid mistake, and the Maritime Union, plus Mr. Rivercombe's supposedly foolproof connections with an ex-FBI man, and Adam's own discovery of two Traceys, made me decide I had better rely on myself for a while. But still, I would need a little help to begin my detecting.

Without waiting for breakfast I hurriedly dressed and took a cab down to the Fisherman's Wharf exhibit. Chato was sweeping around the box office and exterior of the building, but no one else was around. I didn't like to exchange conversation with him because I knew how much he disliked me, though I couldn't figure out why. But there didn't seem to be any alternative.

I went at it directly. After his first sidelong glance at me he began sweeping a little harder, stirring up dust, which wasn't too helpful on a windy day.

"Have you found Tom Tracey's address yet?"

He didn't look up. "No. You?"

I forced myself not to utter the natural remark, "If I knew, would I be asking you?"

I went over to the turnstile and looked in.

"I don't suppose the Chandragars are here yet."

He grunted, but I began to hear rattling, clanking noises high up somewhere in that loft or attic above the four cabin exhibits and guessed Verne was up there working on the machinery.

"May I go in?" I asked Chato, but he had swept himself around the corner of the building by this time, so I reached beyond the end of the turnstile and pressed the button that released it.

I walked along the passage, thinking about the

ships whose fate had produced this horrible but probably fascinating exhibit. I called Verne's name several times but my voice only echoed through the big, barny museum in an eerie way that reminded me of my accident the last time I was in here. I wasn't going to make that mistake again, so I looked around. Nothing dangerous was liable to hit me here.

At the back of the exhibit was the staircase to the loft. I stood at the foot and called, "Verne! Are you up there?"

I had almost given up any idea of talking to him when I saw his tousled dark head looming up against the light from a single bulb in the loft. He grinned.

"Hi! I see the mountain came to Mohammed."

"Thanks. I've never had a more delicate compliment."

"What can I do you for? If I can borrow a fiver from Chato or Ma, how about lunch?"

I was amused. Small wonder Tom Tracey and the Chandragars had found each other. They had the same view of life.

"Let me take you," I offered. "But that's not why I came. Father is still in Reno, isn't he? Have you heard anything more?"

He sat down on the top step, put his chin in the palm of one hand and looked at me soulfully.

"You mean that? This is my lucky day."

"Do I mean what? That Father is in Nevada? But isn't he?"

"I mean—are you going to pick up the lunch tab?"

I laughed. "Right on, man!" and hearing sounds at the front of the exhibits, I started up the steps, speaking in just above a whisper, "Look, Verne! I've got to find Father and get this thing straightened out."

"What thing?" he asked me in a stage whisper.

"About the other—" I broke off. I found sudden perspiration on my upper lip. He apparently knew nothing about the second Thomas Tracey. Or was he just an exceedingly clever actor?

"Nothing. I meant that I want to see Father and help him. Chato says some men are after him about a gambling debt. And he might be in real danger."

Tom Tracey might also find he had escaped, or paid off, his gambling-gangster friends, only to fall into the net that must be thrown about him by Glenn Rivercombe and Adam McKendrick. I hadn't forgotten Rivercombe's telegram mentioning "Prosecution in process." Either way, Father was in serious trouble.

Someone was moving around in one of the exhibits. I didn't want to put myself in the way of another "accidental" jab from a steel rod, so, with reluctance, I moved up the old steps. They made me nervous as I pictured myself rising to the height of that loft.

"Good for you!" Verne reached out a hand to me. "Come up and see my hideaway. Sometimes I sleep up here." At the top of the steps I saw that there were two rooms, no hall or passage, simply one room opening into another beyond. And what rooms! Grubby and dusty, furnished with an incredible collection of pseudo-historic pieces which I took to be discards from other exhibits.

"How do you like it?"

I couldn't tell whether he was joking or not. "You sleep . . . here?" I managed to ask, not committing myself.

"Well, Chato. And sometimes me. Have a seat. No. That's broke. Take this footstool. Tell me now, what's this all about? I take it from Chato that old Tom's really in trouble. I know about the gambling boys. But it's something else, too. Isn't it? Isn't there anything that can be done?"

"I hope so. That's why I'm going up to Reno. Don't you think you could find out where he is from Chato? He might tell you. I'm sure he knows."

Verne ruffled his perennially uncombed hair.

"Yeah. I might. He don't talk much, but I think he kind of likes Tom. Look around. It's a spook haven but it's home to Chato. And to me."

We went in opposite directions, I to the back room, actually over the front of the building, and

Verne to the stairs. At the far end of the second room, low-roofed like the first and smelling of oiled machinery, I saw a little door which opened into the machinery room, a small place full of wheels and engines and gadgets all Greek to me. None of them were running now. I had just turned back to wait for Verne in the room opening off the steps when I heard a terrific thud and a yelp of pain.

I rushed to the top of the steps. Verne lay in a writhing bundle at the bottom of the steps. I climbed down after him as fast as I could. Something crawled across my leg like a fine spider web. I scratched it off with a shudder and knelt beside Verne.

"Are you badly hurt? What happened?"

He sat up with a little help from me. He was looking awfully pale but he managed to grin.

"Nothing busted, but Christ, it hurts! Just pulled a few muscles."

"You could have broken your neck."

He looked up at the steps. "What a dumb-ass trick! I've gone down those steps must be a thousand times and never tripped yet. But I felt that damned cobweb and next thing I knew, I was doubled up."

"Cobweb!"

I got up and went back to the steps. I knelt on one of the lower steps and felt along the rough edges of the boards above. It was hanging there. A simple broken black thread, one end wrapped and knotted around an old, bent nail.

"Here's your cobweb," I told him and held out the thread. "Who is your friend, Verne?" My hand was shaking and I dropped the thread. He found it after scrambling around for several minutes.

He came to no conclusion as he stared at the thread. "Well, I'll be damned!"

I got up again and looked along the central passage between the four ships' cabins. Nobody was in sight, of course, but I didn't have to see anyone. I knew it must be Chato. Who else was around? But what was the sense of it?

"Verne . . ." He looked at me. "Has Chato anything against you?"

"Not that I know of." He was exercizing all the pulled muscles in his left arm and left leg with great vigor. "He's not exactly mad about anybody, but he's not homicidal, so far as I know. Besides, there's nothing that says a thread can't hang from a nail."

"Then it's me."

He stared at me. "You did it? Why?"

"Don't be so stupid! Pay attention! He knew I went up. He expected me to come down."

"But you could've been killed!"

"Now we're communicating," I praised him with a touch of irony. Though how I would prove my theory, I couldn't imagine.

Verne made a fist, stretched his arm and exercized it vigorously. He appeared to be thinking, and from the squint of his eyes and the crease between his brows, it was a severe effort. The result was not a happy one, so far as I was concerned.

"You know, Barb, that thread could've been there for weeks. Months . . . years . . ."

"Centuries," I mocked him, seeing what was coming.

"Well—not quite that long. The place's only been here a few years. But—"

"But let's forget it."

He looked at me with admiration. "Right. Now, are we going to lunch?"

"*We* aren't going anywhere, so forget it!" I stalked away, out of the building, only to pass Mrs. Chandragar beyond the turnstile. She was all teeth as she welcomed me. "How good to see you so early in the day, dear child!"

"And all in one piece," I added, with an edge that she absolutely refused to understand.

"My dear, whatever do you mean?"

I didn't bother to answer that. "You had better go and rescue your son. He just fell down the stairs!"

CHAPTER 11

For one fleeting second the toothy smile faded. Was I imagining it or did Leah accentuate the pronoun when she asked me, "*He* fell down the stairs?"

She hurried past me along the ships' passage. I called after her, "Have you heard from Tom Tracey?"

She turned briefly. "Your father will call me, I am sure. He always has."

"Thank you. Would you leave the name of his Reno hotel or motel at the St. Francis? I want to help him."

"Certainly, my dear child. Or—you might leave anything with me that you want him to have and I can see that he gets it. I imagine this is just another little financial problem he must work out. It won't be the first time I have—as we say—bailed him out. So it might be simpler all around if I took charge of whatever was to be used to help him."

"We'll talk about that later," I lied, not wanting to get her off me permanently. I might need her later to help me with Tom Tracey. But I had no intention of giving her money on the slim chance that she would see that he got it.

"If I know Tom," she went on, "he won't call until after six."

"Has he been to Reno before? Where does he usually stay?"

"When he is in the chips, as he calls it, he stays at the Holiday or the Riverside, or a motel near the Riverside. . . . Or did he mention Harrah's last time? Well, no matter. He is not at any of those places this time. Excuse me, please. Verne, where are you?"

Verne limped into sight and came toward her, still vigorously exercizing his arms, first one, then the other. He reassured his mother with a quick punching motion before calling to me.

"Got to get those stairs swept, Ma. Wait up, Barb. I've got a great idea. Hold on a sec."

He passed his mother, who stared after him with what even I considered justifiable confusion as he limped to me.

"Go and put a—put a band-aid on your leg!" I told him rudely, but he made a grab for my arm as

I moved out onto the sidewalk. He was exactly like a small, mischievous boy. It was hard to be cross with him just because he refused to admit that his fall had been a deliberate attempt to break my neck. Or in any event, my leg.

"Barb, you going up to Reno?"

"To look for Tom Tracey, yes. He can use a little help. Even your mother thinks so."

"I've got my T-Bird. Been out of hock almost a week. Let me drive you up to Reno. I have a few ideas where he might hole up." I was thinking this over when he added the clincher that somehow made me trust his offer. "That is, if you'll stand the gas, and—" he added hopefully, "—lunch?"

"Why not?"

I could almost read his mini-calculator mind. "And—look, Barb, if we have to spend the night there—"

"What!"

"No, no! I meant . . . could you stand my tab? I mean—I'll be doing this for you. And for old Tom, natch."

"Natch!" But I had to break down and laugh. There was no getting around this young golddigger. Besides, the knowledge that I had left town to do some detecting on my own, or worse, with Verne Chandragar, ought to shake up Adam McKendrick and my Chicago boss who, between them, couldn't even be sure who was the real Tom Tracey.

We agreed to meet outside my hotel in an hour and I called a cab and hurried back to pack an overnight bag. Adam had left a message which he nicely labelled "urgent." Oddly enough, there was a call from Rose Cortapassi. That one I returned. She came on the line after a little delay.

"Good morning, Barbara-Jane. Please excuse my tardiness. I am in the middle of preparations for dinner. Manicotti. And my hands were full of pasta and spinach. I wonder if you remember. It was the only way your father said you would eat spinach." She laughed, a self-deprecating, pleasant laugh that made me think suddenly of long ago, of the young Cortapassis, and of Father. I did remember the sound of her laughter and the taste of her heavenly Manicotti.

"That sounds divine, Mrs. Cortapassi. I can almost smell it from here."

"You are kind."

"You left your number; so I called."

"Ah! Of course. Yes. I called earlier. I was cleaning your father's room and I found something which might interest you. Pictures your father had saved, from your young days. They are not in color. Only black and white. It was before the popularity of color snapshots. I would say the pictures are dated—" She probably looked on the back of the picture nearest her and said, after a beat or two, "—1950. Yes."

I thought with a sinking feeling: *They are sure*

to be evidence in favor of the Cortapassis' Thomas Tracey, and I don't want him nor his evidence.

But aloud I said, "Thank you so much. I do want to see the snapshots. Unfortunately, I'll be gone the rest of the day. I'll see you tomorrow if I can."

"You will be gone? But—you are not interested in seeing this proof of . . . ? Pardon. It is your concern. Only poor Thomas is hoping so much that you will believe in him. When I mentioned the value of these snapshots—"

"I'm sorry. Tomorrow, for sure."

She sighed, then perked up. "That is good. He will be happy tonight, thinking of tomorrow."

Whatever the Cortapassis may hope or believe, I thought, *I know who my father is, and he's not that poor devil living in back of the Cortapassis' garage.*

Why I should be so snobbish and prefer a man in hiding from Las Vegas gambling men, obviously a man who couldn't pay his debts and had run out, I didn't know. But I still felt that the father I remembered from my childhood was the Tom Tracey whom I was going off, perhaps half-cocked, to help if I could.

I said "thank you" again to Rose Cortapassi and we both rang off.

Unfortunately, as I changed rapidly for the trip over the Sierras, I felt guilty at deceiving the Cortapassis. They meant well, were generous and good-hearted, and I was making every effort to destroy their belief in the imposter for whom they had done so much.

I was just changing the contents of my small suede shoulder-bag to a larger travel handbag when I came across the nail file I had once used to puncture a would-be mugger. I thought of Verne Chandrager, my escort, about whom I knew so little. Of course, his best argument for driving me, instead of letting me catch a plane by myself, was that he might know more than I about Tom Tracey's hangouts in Reno. I also admitted that since I loathed planes and the heights they always conjured up to add to my phobia, I was choosing the easy way out by letting Verne drive me. I was doing something foolhardy. At the same time I had the utmost confidence that I could handle him. If common sense and my sharp temper failed, he still struck me as a young man who could be bribed out of any violent notions he might have.

I showed up on time in front of the hotel but, unlike Adam McKendrick, Verne was not the prompt sort. I grew more and more uncertain of my decision as I waited, wondering why I had trusted a fellow who had probably never done an honest day's work and would simply be a nuisance demanding money every hour on the trip. But presently, when I had given him up and was turning back to my makeup-and-overnight case which stood beside the doorman, I saw the doorman's quick smile of recognition. I swung around, surprised that he knew the old T-Bird I was waiting for, and saw Adam McKendrick getting out of his golden yellow Chrysler.

As always, the sight of him affected me—my glands—in a maddening way, and I knew from his expression that he had seen my case and that he didn't like what it suggested. I tried to be on my best behavior, but frankly, I was nervous. I kept hoping that as long as Verne was this late, he would be a little later.

"Good morning, darling." As I raised my eyes he added with a little haste and uneasiness that warmed and delighted me, "—er—Barbara. Going somewhere?"

When he saw my smile he reached for me. We kissed in spite of the interested audience on the sidewalk and under the canopy. I was not going to miss this chance, whatever the furor which was bound to arise when he heard that I was going away without telling him my plans and certainly without betraying my destination. After all, he shared Mr. Rivercombe's ambition to put Tom Tracey in jail! He would love to have me lead him right to my father.

"Now then," he held me away from him by my shoulders and looked me up and down. "What are you up to?"

"What do you mean—up to? I'm . . . well, I'm just going for the day, to look up somebody who used to know me when I was a child. I thought it might clear up some of our problems."

"Wonderful! Who is it? Did you give us the name when we began the investigation? Or is it someone you just thought of? We can check her out immediately."

. . . *I'll bet!* . . .

I said more hurriedly than I would have liked, "I believe I told Mr. Rivercombe, but I may have told you when I first arrived in San Francisco. Anyway, I do have to go now. I'll call you when I return, if you like."

"Fine. I'll drive you out to the airport." Adam was ominously cheerful as he took my arm and started toward his car. It didn't help matters that the doorman held out my case, as though he wanted to cooperate in this genteel kidnapping.

I dragged back. "No! Look! I'm not—that is, you have your work to do. I'd like you to examine the background of that man we met last night. Mrs. Cortapassi called today. I think it's something important. Don't worry about me. Run along and find out what it's all about with Mrs. Cortapassi."

"And I'll see you for dinner?"

"Of course."

As we stood by his car, he looked down at me, smiling pleasantly, and said, "You liar!"

I opened my mouth, tried to show my true

indignation, but couldn't make the righteous denial this accusation demanded. I felt very deeply my own ambiguous position. I was lying, but in a good cause. I had to see and talk to Tom Tracey, and help if I could, before I could be fully candid with Adam, who had placed himself flatly against my own Tom Tracey.

"Think what you like. I'm not trying to censor your thoughts." And I added in a flurry, ". . . Which is exactly what you tried to do to me."

He rolled his eyes heavenward.

"Female logic! Why do they always twist everything around to make us guilty?"

Behind him I saw Verne drive his white and slightly battered Thunderbird gently into the license plate of Adam's car. Startled, Adam turned and stared.

"What the devil?"

"Oh, there's my ride. Call me tonight . . . darling," I cried and rushed up toward the white car.

"About time!" I told Verne who was all smiles as he reached over and unlocked the door. I got in and looked back, waving to Adam. He didn't seem to see me. He was returning to his car in front of us. This fact didn't make me any friendlier to the exceedingly late Verne Chandragar.

"Why?" he asked innocently. "Or am I late?"

I looked daggers, but it was true. He didn't

wear a wrist watch and I couldn't picture him with any other timepiece tucked away. I wondered if he had put his watch in hock, which seemed to be his custom about anything of value.

"You were late. And unfortunately I was seen out here waiting for you."

Verne grinned. "Yeah. I saw. The big shot looks like he's got a thing going for you. Must be nice to be tall, bright, handsome and rich."

"Don't be silly," I said, softening a little under his heavy—and probably fake—humility. But as we drove past Adam, who was starting his car, I tried to catch Adam's attention. He did glance my way, but I could hardly miss the frigid look that can be particularly devastating in blue-eyed men. Anyway, it couldn't be helped. Some day, maybe he would understand. Verne saw me frowning and guessed at once what caused it.

"Lovers' quarrel?"

"We are not amused."

He tried to liven things up conversationally, but it was a one-sided affair, and I'm afraid the first section of our drive was a total loss for him. Well, not a total loss. I paid to have the gas tank filled up when we had crossed the Bay Bridge and were headed inland toward Martinez, and Verne, being told by the enterprising station attendant that we needed oil, looked at me expectantly. I agreed and a quart of oil was added to the first expenses on the trip.

"Cost you a lot more for air fare," Verne reminded me.

"I'm not complaining."

"That guy really gets to you; don't he?"

I was not foolish enough to think he was referring to the station attendant, but I didn't let myself get upset over it. I said evenly, "Attend to your driving and I'll attend to my business."

He grinned and after a few minutes began chattering again about how well he and I got along. Since he wasn't saying anything that interested me much, I had no hesitation in interrupting him.

"What did you or your mother know about Tom before he and your mother became . . . partners?"

"You mean lovers. Anyway, he was a hanger-on around the docks. And Hawaii. We checked him out." He glanced at me. "Still doing the oh-oh-seven bit? He's level, you know."

I reminded him that we were headed onto the bridge high over the Carquinez Straits, not a place to be driving blind. He took my advice but asked in an unexpectedly tense voice, "Somebody put you onto these new doubts?"

I think I was less troubled by the direct question than by his tone, so mature and sharp. It reminded me that he was not really just a tousle-headed young drifter, a simple-minded gigolo. What else was he?

"Who said I had doubts? I wouldn't be going up

to Reno looking for Father if I had doubts. I suppose you'll want money for the bridge toll. How much?"

"Not 'til we're inbound on the other bridge over there."

I didn't look the way he pointed. I was very conscious of the change in the atmosphere and hurriedly tried to lull his suspicions.

"The reason I asked you is because I want to know everything about Tom, so there won't be any awful blanks between us. We were apart for so long—it seemed so unfair to him. Letting him wander all over the world when Mother could have made things easier for him. Now, I intend to make it right with poor Father."

To my surprise this friend of Tom Tracey's, the son of Tom's mistress, reminded me drily, "You can bet he wanted to wander if he wandered. You've got nothing to feel guilty about. Maybe your Ma, but I never knew her. Can't say I missed anything, not knowing her. Sorry."

"Don't mention it." But I wasn't upset, except by the unexpectedness of his remark. I could have sworn he would jump to Tom Tracey's defense, especially urging me to make financial restitution in some way.

The freeway gave Verne a chance to make good time, and once we reached the High Sierra ridges, still rimmed with spring snow beneath the pines,

Verne began to describe the famous ski runs of the area. I shivered but he went rambling on.

"You'd love the runs. But with your money I guess you could go any place. How do the Austrian and Swiss runs stack up with the ones at home?"

"I wouldn't know!"

He looked at me curiously. "What's the matter? Allergic to snow?"

"No. To heights. I don't even like this altitude."

"Well, I'll be damned! Why not?"

I started. "Because I don't like high places. Ski runs, elevators, high trams, any of those things."

Verne was still puzzled. "That's a funny one. I know some bunnies don't like tight places, elevators, stuff like that, but it's nothing to do with ski runs and mountains. It's usually because they've had an accident, or got stuck in an elevator. Something like that. But a nice, normal chick like you . . . Why would you have a complex?"

I sat there thinking: Only two people seemed to know about my elevator accident. Adam didn't know, and Verne didn't know; yet both my "fathers" knew, though I couldn't imagine how. I was completely mystified.

I got out of the conversation by agreeing with Verne, who promptly changed the subject and told me he had once had a terrific run of luck at roulette in one of the casinos in Reno and he felt lucky today, "If I just had a stake."

"We're going to find Tom Tracey. You can try for your stake some other day."

"You're a hard woman!" But he didn't persist. He was disconcerting, however, when he remarked suddenly, "You call him Tom most of the time now. What happened to dear old 'Dad?' "

I bit my lips. He was pretty bright, not dumb at all. "I suppose because he doesn't seem like dear old Dad. He's too vigorous and vital." It was a lie, because I had always thought of my father as vigorous and vital, and I couldn't have told myself, much less Verne, why I was no longer calling Tom Tracey *father*.

At a little after two in the afternoon we drove off the freeway into Reno which looked what it was, a busy little western cattle and ranching town, rather surprised to find three or four skyscrapers suddenly blossoming out of vacant lots and ancient wooden hotels that had known the glory of Golden Tonopah and the silver of Virginia City.

"It isn't very big," I said. "Surely, we could cover all the hotels this afternoon."

He laughed abruptly. "You aren't counting the fifty million motels and a couple of guest ranches, though I can't see old Tom cuddling up in one of them. Unless he wants to upset Ma. Too many tempting divorcees." As I thought this over, he looked up at the rear-view mirror. "But then, of course, our guardian angels might spot him. That should help somebody."

"What do you mean?" I looked around. Several cars were following us but the one immediately behind us was hardly a threat. It was a black Volkswagen. "That one?"

"Probably the yellow one behind it. See if it follows us." He turned sharply at the shabby street facing on the east-west railroad tracks. The yellow car did not follow us. It moved on through the block of gambling casinos and we lost it.

"Wasn't that the color of your boyfriend's car?"

"Nothing like it," I lied. I was getting adept at lies. Because, of course, it was the color of Adam's car. But it had passed us. The little black Volkswagen, however, had turned off behind us. We decided to park the car in a lot a couple of blocks from the casino section of town since Verne claimed to have several ideas of motels where Tom Tracey occasionally stayed.

"Has he done this often, run away from gambling debts in order to gamble some more and pay them off?"

Verne shrugged. "Once or twice." He looked after the black Volkswagen which disappeared in the distance. "Looks like we can rule that out." Then he turned to more important matters. "Don't you think we can work better on full stomachs?"

Poor fellow! He probably was sincere about

that, at least. I promised we would eat after we had tried a couple of places. "And after we've called your mother."

There was a telephone booth in the first motel, and after we checked and found neither Tom Tracey nor Thomas Michaels was registered, Verne called his mother. Leah Chandragar reported from the Fisherman's Wharf exhibit that she had heard nothing from Tom but that two males who looked like businessmen and drove a respectable Oldsmobile with a Clark County, Nevada license plate, were asking for Tom. Verne and I exchanged glances.

"Sounds bad," Verne acknowledged, and without any pleasantries except "Thanks, Ma. Keep cool," he hung up.

"We've got to hurry," I said anxiously. "Shall we separate? We can cover more places locally."

"No. I just thought of a place where he stayed once, and said it was a great hideout. A little-nothing auto court on the way to Sparks. It's been around since—well, practically since the year one. We'll get the car and . . ." He had lost the thread of his conversation. There was a bundle of Reno afternoon newspapers just in the rack, and the front page of the paper had attracted his attention. He caught his breath. I leaned over, examined the front page. The right-hand column reported the discovery of a drowned man in the reeds of the

Truckee River within a hundred yards of the Kietzke Lane overpass.

"About fifty-six," Verne read aloud. "Six feet tall . . . graying red hair . . . silver belt buckle with initials T.M.T. . . ."

I cried out something. Verne grabbed my arm, shook me. I closed my eyes. Father's enemies must have reached him before we got here.

"The gamblers!" I whispered. "They murdered him!"

Verne took up the paper. "How could it be the gamblers? Mother was talking to them only a couple of hours ago. This happened early this morning, it says here. Besides, Tom didn't wear any Silver buckle. What the devil does it mean?"

CHAPTER 12

After Verne had called and arranged the ghastly business of identifying Tom Tracey, he suggested, "While we're waiting, we ought to clear up about where he stayed the last couple of nights. If they did do him in, there should be some evidence, some signs. Wouldn't you say?"

"I suppose so." I was too sick and discouraged to say much. We sat in Verne's car drinking cold Cokes because Verne said I looked ready to cave in and the Coke box was handiest. I wasn't ready to cave in. I kept remembering that I had seen a car like Adam's behind us, that Adam was going to "prosecute" Tom Tracey, and Adam believed Tom Tracey was a fake.

Did I actually believe Adam McKendrick was capable of such a crime? Ridiculous! It was sure to have been the gamblers. But I wished I hadn't seen signs of Adam's presence in Reno. It might even have caused Tom Tracey to take fright and drown himself, although the present river flow here on the threshold of summer certainly didn't look as if it would drown a full-grown man. And Father had always been an excellent swimmer. But then, if the dead man was my Tom Tracey, what would he be doing in the river, unless he had been put there?

Verne said suddenly, "Look here. We've got an hour before we can get into their morgue to identify it."

"Don't call him *it!*"

He made a quick, chopping motion. "Okay-okay. I didn't mean it like it sounds. But this whole thing smells."

"Of course it does. It's murder!"

"I didn't mean that. Never mind. The point is, why don't we try a couple of downtown motels where he's stayed in the past? Afterward, we can call the others."

"But why? I don't understand."

"Because," he explained patiently, "whoever killed him—if that's what happened—might have visited him there and we could get the description. Something for the police to go on."

It made sense. "We could drive out to that place you mentioned on the road to—where on earth is Sparks?"

"Slap up against Reno. They've got a big casino in Sparks but he wouldn't have stayed there. Not if he didn't want to be found. No, it might be the old place. The Easy—no—the Comfort Auto Court. I'll call there, then clear with the other locals."

We got out of the car. There was a public telephone in the small, we-carry-everything grocery on the corner across the street. We headed for it while Verne reminded me that he would need several dimes. Fortunately, I was able to oblige. I looked up the number in the small, neat city telephone book. It appeared to be within the dialing zone. Verne tried.

"Don't they answer?" I asked after several seconds.

He shook his head. "Maybe the whole tribe is dead—"

"Verne!"

"—drunk." He hung up, his face corrugated by his frown. "Hey! Never mind the other places. I've got a hunch about this one. How long have we got before the appointment with the fuzz?"

"Fifty minutes."

"Let's go. We can get there in five minutes. Ten if the traffic is bad."

We hurried back to the car. Either Verne Chandragar was trying to please me in the hope of making a little money, or he genuinely cared about his mother's lover. Or . . . he was deeply curious for some secret reason of his own.

How suspicious I was getting lately! But for twenty years I had been forced back upon myself, alone but not lonely. Finding my own pleasure. Had I ever really trusted anyone since Mother and I left Father? Adam McKendrick maybe. And perhaps Mr. Rivercombe and my Chicago fellow workers. And the legal-eagles in San Francisco who had drawn up my will. But no one else. Why should I trust Verne Chandragar, who might be part of a vile conspiracy of some kind?

I sat quietly in the car as we drove along the street that bisected Reno and Sparks, linking both with U.S. Highway 80. I was surprised to see the many tree-lined side streets. I had never linked all this greenery with a town famed for divorce and gambling. The afternoon had grown very warm, almost stifling. Or else I was getting more nervous by the minute.

Near the city line we came to a series of little wooden cottages almost hidden by rustling cottonwood trees of impressive size. The cottages were old but well-made and all freshly painted white with green trim. Not the drab, depressing place I had expected.

"Better not leave the car until I find out what's cooking," Verne suggested.

"You expect those gangsters to come slamming out with all barrels blazing?"

He ignored my gallows humor. I watched him walk up the three wooden steps to the screen door of the front bungalow. A weathered sign indicated that the manager would return at three P.M. Presumably, he was in. Verne pressed the buzzer. The door seemed to be ajar behind the screen because when Verne got no answer, he pushed open the door and disappeared inside.

I waited anxiously, biting my nails, then angry with myself for resorting to such a childish release. But for just a minute or two there had been something marvelously comfortable about leveling off the nail and proceeding to do a neat job on the next . . . and the next. When I was a child, only Father could stop me after I started this nervously satisfying habit. He had merely looked at my hands, told me how "small and well-shaped" they were, "And a bloody shame it is to *uglify* them this way. You fail yourself, Accushla."

During all the years since, I had not bitten my nails. I remembered too well Father's flattery about my hands, the clever appeal to my pride. But now, here I was resorting to that baby trick again, as if his influence could no longer prevent me from "failing myself."

I got out of the car and walked to the manager's bungalow. I was just thinking of going up the steps after Verne when he and an ancient female came out, Verne gallantly holding the screen door open for her. She may have been ancient but she was far from senile.

"Lot of charm, that boy," she was saying.

It sounded odd to hear my father called "that boy," but then, the charm didn't surprise me at all.

With a sudden, terrible premonition that we would find an empty cottage, I called out, "Does she know him? Was he here?"

"I know Mister Michaels," the old lady told me crossly. "He was here early last night. Went out to try his luck at the clubs. Don't know what time he got in, but he sounds like your boy, all right."

Verne nodded to me and we followed the old lady to one of the bungalows at the back of the horseshoe-shaped little group of wooden buildings. They all seemed to possess no more than two small rooms and a bathroom, but they looked pleasant in the shade of those huge cottonwoods and some lesser foliage.

The old manager pressed the buzzer outside the screen door. When nothing happened she opened the screen and knocked. We stood below the steps waiting, Verne and I. I don't know what Verne's state of mind was, but I felt faint and my knees were shaky. I knew we were going to discover the worst: an empty bungalow. The old lady reached into the pocket of her crisply starched Hoover apron and pulled out a big ring of keys. There was a terrific rattle and clanking noise.

"Like opening dungeon doors," Verne murmured sotto-voce.

I didn't smile. I was too nervous, too anxious.

The old lady looked around at us.

"Seems to be an obstacle. Something or other. Give me that strong shoulder of yours, boy."

Verne leaped up the stairs, put his shoulder to the door with its ring of keys still dangling from the lock, and at the same time I saw a shadow move behind the warped Venetian blinds.

"Someone is in there!" I cried out, and then thought . . . *It's sure to be a cleaning woman. A janitor. Someone working* . . .

But as Verne pushed against the door there was a metallic clicking sound inside. A safety chain being removed. That was why the door was stuck. I held my breath. Verne bounded head first into the room. The old lady shuffled in after him.

Over their heads, looming out of the room's shadowy obscurity, I saw the rough, graying red hair and the humorous yet curiously unreadable eyes of my Tom Tracey. They looked far from humorous now, but I was so relieved, yet so shocked, I stood there shaking, unable to get up the steps.

Verne had stumbled back against the old lady when he caught sight of my father.

"Jesus Christ, Tom! What are you trying to pull?"

Tom Tracey looked behind us, out at the gravel and the busy highway beyond the front bungalows. It was clear to me, as I recovered my common sense and watched him, that he was afraid, half-expecting that those gamblers were coming to collect their money . . . or kill him? It seemed highly melodramatic, but then, the whole business was melodramatic.

Tom satisfied himself that we weren't the harbingers of what he dreaded, and flashed his big, remembered smile at me.

"Come in, Sprout. Come in. You look tuckered out. Thanks for bringing them to me, Mrs. Baynes. Come in, both of you. Let me know what's going on in the big world outside."

The old lady was reluctant but he clearly didn't include her in his invitation, so she shuffled back down the steps and left us after a last warning: "No funny business, now!"

"Whatever that means," Verne muttered, shaking his head. He motioned me toward the little bungalow.

When I reached him I whispered, "I don't understand any of this. Who is the man they found in the Truckee River?"

Verne shrugged. "Some poor guy whose luck ran out. Maybe he just did it himself. A suicide."

"He couldn't have drowned in that trickle of water. Maybe in early spring but not now. I tell you—"

"Watch it! Well, Tom, I think you've got some explaining to do."

Tom Tracey closed the door behind Verne and put up the chain.

"You kids gave me a scare. How the hell did you find me? Not that I'm not mighty glad to see you. Look here, did either of you see any suspicious-looking jokers hanging around the office up front?"

It was all shadowy in the room. He had every Venetian blind shut with only an inch or two of afternoon sunlight trickling through.

"Drink?" Tom asked. " 'Fraid it's got to be bourbon. I was a little short. Had some luck last night, though. One more good shot at those crap tables and I'll be able to cover that business in Vegas. Trouble is, I have to play the dinky little one-shot places. Can't be seen in the big casinos."

I refused the drink but Verne took it, in a cracked water glass. He didn't drink much. He was looking at Tom Tracey with the same dumbfounded, and not entirely trusting expression that I felt must mirror my own feelings.

"Have you any idea what's been going on? Don't you read the papers?"

"What's that got to do with the price of eggs? Of course, I read the papers." Tom Tracey threw a *San Francisco Chronicle* into Verne's lap. "Got it this morning when I came in off the crap tables."

Silently, Verne gave him the folded *Reno Evening Gazette*. He looked over the front page, missed the article, then went back to it.

"Holy Mother of God!" His long legs gave out. He sat down abruptly beside me on the faded and lumpy couch. He put out one hand, squeezed mine reassuringly. "It sure isn't me."

I still found the relief partially obliterated by dreadful, secret questions.

"But the initials. The silver belt with your initials!"

He shrugged, looked from me to Verne who was studying him in an uncomfortably serious way.

"Verne knows I don't have a belt like that. Not my speed. I—I don't know what to say. Except it isn't your old father, Barby. You don't think—" He glanced quickly at the chain on the door. "Good God! You don't think this guy could've been mistaken for me and—"

"Not likely," Verne reminded him. "Gamblers don't kill their pigeons. Scare them, sure, but why drown the guy? Besides, he'd have to look like you."

"I came up here to help you, Father," I said, cutting into their murder speculation. "They're not going to kill you if you pay them."

Some of the tension lifted from his craggy face. He got up and went to the window, looked out between the slats.

"Wouldn't that solve it?" Verne asked.

Tom Tracey was still squinting to see the distant street.

"The thing is, how to get the word to them. I could call a pit boss I know in Vegas. It's a kind of private place, not one of the big clubs. You think anyone could've followed you two kids?"

Verne cut this off impatiently. "Christ, Tom! Get with it! You're not making a thirties gangster movie. These guys are businessmen. They're after your payment, not your scalp."

"Then what about the dead guy in the river?"

"What about it? It could be anybody. Anyway, we're on our way in a couple of minutes to see if we can identify it, though now—" Verne looked at me. "—is there any point to it? I mean, we're bound not to know the poor guy. And you don't want to go through anything like that for a stranger. We're not going to find two guys like old Tom here. Twins don't grow on trees."

Dear God! I thought. *Is there a twin to this Tom Tracey? A man who looks enough like him so that the description in the paper, and the initials might fit him . . .*

I swallowed my revulsion at the idea and I said, "I've got to. It may be no use for you, Verne. I don't think you would know him. But I have to be sure."

Verne and Tom Tracey stared at me. Verne voiced what was obviously their mutual question: "You know who this poor joker might be?"

"I hope not." I looked at Tom Tracey, who was scowling. "Do you know? Do you know anyone else in the world, for instance, who might want to find you?" As he stiffened and obviously began to remember the danger he was in, I added, "To arrest you . . . Father?"

"You mean the Vegas boys? Frankly, you may as well know, Sprout, they don't have a legal leg to stand on, even in Nevada. And if I pay them off . . ."

Verne appeared to be out of this and thoroughly confused. "What's this all about? Why are those jokers trying to kill you if they'll settle for money? Then they had no reason to kill the poor devil in the river. In fact, we don't even know he was murdered. Just a wino, maybe. Fell in, cracked his head. Anything."

I said, "How much is your debt?"

Verne studied Tom Tracey, who grinned and looked ingratiating, exactly the way he—or was it he?—had looked years ago when Mother accused him of failing us in some way. In my memory, as I looked back now, he had always tried to please us in one way or another, though never about holding a responsible job. The Cortapassis' Thomas Tracey was a little like that.

"Well, hon, it's a little over eleven thousand after I pay off the three thousand I've made here."

I heard Verne's sharp intake of breath, but he didn't interfere. As for the amount, I wasn't surprised. I said, "I can give you—maybe four thousand in a check. I can get the rest tomorrow in San Francisco. Then will you be safe?"

"He'll be safe," Verne cut in coldly. "We're going to be late to that medical center, or whatever it is. Coming, Barb?"

I started to make out the check but Tom Tracey stopped me. "Hon, might be hard for me to cash a check in this town. Could you—possibly—get me the cash?"

I was crisp and businesslike. He might use this cash to gamble. He might still be in danger afterward. But that would be a whole new ballgame and I would turn it over to Mr. Rivercombe. Aloud, I said, "All right. And I know you'll have all this settled. If you can't settle it, then you'll be much safer if we let Mr. Rivercombe and Mr. McKendrick, or maybe Mr. Merritte, my local lawyer, handle it for you."

If I had been in a cheerful mood, I would have laughed at the flicker of distress that crossed Tom's mobile face. He licked his lips a bit nervously.

"I give you my word, Sprout, I'll handle it. I'll make the call tonight. But can't you two stay a little longer? Have another drink? Verne, let me top that drink of yours."

But we both refused. When we left Tom Tracey kissed me on the cheek and gave me a quick hug. I couldn't help hugging him back. He looked so woebegone, I assured him at the last, "You'll be all right, Father. They wouldn't dare do anything to an ancient leprechaun like you."

This brought out his familiar grin.

"I wasn't thinking money, for once. Take good care of her, boy."

"Ay, ay, ancient leprechaun!"

So we parted friends.

We drove back into downtown Reno, lost our way among the tree-lined streets with their old-fashioned stucco houses and a few amusing Victorian wooden "mansions" that reminded me of San Francisco. I had never dreaded anything so much as this business of trying to identify a dead man, even though I kept reminding myself that my greatest fear of his identity was over now. He couldn't be Tom Tracey, nor anyone else I knew.

Anyone?

We walked in through the rear entrance and along what seemed to me endless white corridors, passing white uniformed workers who didn't look the least like those friendly, human characters I had seen so often on television. To my highly charged imagination they all wore masks, indifferent, inhuman. I became more and more nervous. Verne gave our names at the desk and I was surprised when we were escorted to the elevator and a room in what was either the basement or a more elegant lower level. I had expected uniformed policemen but instead there were a man and woman whose identity I never did discover. They were both in hospital whites, and they seemed to regard us with the practical but inhuman competence that made me sentimental over what I considered this indifference to a dead man.

I had been worried for fear we would have to see other bodies in "showcases," as Verne had helpfully described the old San Francisco morgue, since replaced. But there was only one sheeted body under a light I found much too bright, though Verne assured me later that I had imagined half of what we saw, especially the atmosphere. Nevertheless, it was Verne who pushed me forward as they rolled back the cover, and in a matter of three or four seconds it was all over and done. I looked down at the face, colorless, yet veined like marbled wax, with a couple of scratches on the left temple. There were the liver spots I remembered, oddly now, with tenderness. His wrinkles and tired look were all smoothed out in death, making him much younger than when I last saw him.

He was my . . . he was the Cortapassis' Thomas Tracey.

Verne had to take several steps forward and back before he could move up to the impassive pair presenting all that remained of that unhappy and pitiful man I had met for the first time at the Cortapassis'. But was it the first time?

Verne took one quick look, then backed up again and joined me, shaking his head.

"Never saw him before. Let's go."

He was already halfway out the door when I looked back at the doctor and nurse. The doctor asked me without any expectation of an answer, "And you, Miss Tracey?"

There was a painful lump in my throat and my voice sounded odd, unfamiliar to me when I answered, "Yes. I know him."

Afterward, I made endless reports, talked to endless people, although Verne, fascinated by the idea of another Thomas Tracey, assured me later that I exaggerated. I gave Mr. and Mrs. Alfredo Cortapassi as those who should be immediately concerned, and although I gave what I vaguely remembered as their address, I didn't recall the phone number.

All my brain kept saying to me was *Why? Why? Why?*

Because, to tell the truth, I didn't really believe "my other father" died in the Truckee River by accident, nor from the effects of a blow by those Vegas gamblers pursuing Tom Tracey. We learned one thing in return for my information. Thomas Tracey, that sad, eager, would-be father of mine, had died not from drowning but from a blow at the back of the head, which may, or may not have occurred when he presumably fell down the embankment of the river. He had smelled to high heaven of gin, they said, so it was obvious that he had fallen because he was drunk.

While I remained in town preparing a laboriously full report on all facts I knew about the dead Thomas Tracey, Verne took the money I managed to get just before the banks closed their doors at five o'clock that Friday. Tom Tracey was lucky it was Friday. But meanwhile, and in spite of my doubts and suspicions, I did not tell the Reno police about Tom Tracey and his presence in town. I did discuss the search for my father, and gave the names of Adam McKendrick, Glenn Rivercombe and my San Francisco legal firm, in case they wanted to investigate the matter. I had the most curious feeling, however, that they knew everything I told them and were only checking on me somehow. I couldn't figure it out, and gave up. There were too many other things to worry about.

Having also given my own addresses, Chicago and San Francisco, I was allowed to leave just as Verne returned from having left the money with Tom Tracey.

"He was kind of disappointed. Said he'd hoped to see you again before you left."

"Tough," I said in a tone that made him look at me in surprise. "Did you tell him about the man in the morgue?"

He hesitated. "No. Wasn't any of his business,

even if the guy did look like him. I just said I didn't know who it was. True enough, as far as I'm concerned."

For the next few minutes, as we got into the car and headed out of this green oasis in the great Nevada desert, Verne tried to eat a sandwich he had thoughtfully provided for himself. Between bites, he kept pursuing the matter of Tom Tracey, and as a sideline, "That dead guy looked enough like old Tom to be—"

"Old Tom?" I asked ironically. "Yes. He did."

He glanced at me several times. "You crying?"

"No. It's the altitude. I hate this altitude!"

He gave up. We began to climb higher and higher into the Sierra night. I huddled down in my seat, trying not to think about the enormous heights of the sawtooth ridges ahead and the big drop below the highway once we passed above Donner Summit which lay below us now on the old, closed highway.

"Heights!" I exclaimed. "I do hate them!"

Verne looked a little more cheerful. "So she can talk, after all." He was driving fast, but I was as anxious as he to get back to San Francisco. The eastbound highway, sometimes below us, was busy, mostly with California cars heading for a fun-and-games weekend at Tahoe or Reno. We seemed to have the wide westbound highway pretty much to ourselves as dusk dissolved into a kind of half-dark, with the western sky still faintly tinted. The highway itself was lined on one side with pines on a steep slope; the other side, my side of the car, overlooked a heart-stopping plunge to the forest carpet that lined a wild, inaccessible canyon.

Presently, though, there were cars behind us. Two or three, matching our speed, passed us. To avoid them we were forced onto the outer rim of the highway.

"Please, slow up a little," I said. "It's pretty nerve-wracking at this speed." It wasn't like him, actually. He was a slower driver than Adam, by far.

"Sorry. I'm trying to lose the little bug behind us."

"What!" I twisted around. I could hardly believe it, but a black Volkswagen seemed to be on our tail. Was this the same car that had followed us on our trip to Reno earlier in the day? "What could they want with us?"

"We picked them up at the Quarantine Station when we had that wait. Probably it's old Tom's gambling friends sore at you for helping Tom pay them off. Maybe they've put out a contract on us."

"Don't be funny!"

It was absurd, but chilling. The "little bug" kept edging closer. I thought it was trying to pass us. There was certainly room enough. Further behind the Volkswagen were several cars, another Volkswagen, this one baby blue, and several larger American cars, one of them a deep, yellow-gold, the color of Adam McKendrick's Chrysler. Not that there weren't thousands of others that color!

"Damned idiot! What's with him?" Verne wanted to know.

I thought for a second he was talking about the yellow car, but, of course, it was the black Volkswagen that bothered him. It kept coming up on our left rear wheel, slipping back, pulling forward.

"Some juvenile with a sense of humor," I suggested, but it was scary to see how the idiot kept approaching, each time closer, before falling back. And each time we were driven closer to the edge.

There were barriers here and there, rocks, slopes of red, dusty earth, but always the other places beyond the earth and rock shoulders. The space, sheer space, how far down? It gave me a headache to think of it. I tried not to look out of the window on my side.

"Can't we get rid of him?"

Verne speeded up. For a few minutes I thought we were going to outrun the black bug, but then it came on, so suddenly Verne had to swerve hard toward the shoulder of the road. I screamed and then, ashamed, tried to stifle the sound. Verne swore and the car leaped ahead. I held on.

The black bug darted at us again. I couldn't make out the driver. I could tell that Verne was squinting, trying to make out a face behind the wheel in that dark little interior. It was like a hideous little weapon aimed at us.

"Christ!" Verne swerved, barely in time. The pursuing car would have rammed along our full length. We hurtled onto the bumpy shoulder. A hundred feet ahead the shoulder fell off into the night-blue Sierra space. We rocked on toward that oblivion.

CHAPTER 13

The black car must have rushed over the highway and out of sight. I only know we hit a submerged rock about ten feet before the edge, and Verne brought the car to a jerking, teeth-rattling stop.

We sat there shaking. I rubbed my neck and shoulders. Verne was nursing the same elbow he had struck early in the day when he fell down the steps of the museum exhibit.

Cars passed. Half a dozen. None stopped. But then lights gleamed through the rear window and a car pulled up and stopped behind us. I twisted around painfully. It was Adam's yellow Chrysler. I could hardly mistake his tall figure, nor his hair, bronze in the car lights. I cried his name but I didn't dare to move or to open my door. The car was hardly more than a couple of feet from the edge, on my side.

Very gently, and before he asked any questions, Adam opened the door on Verne's side and half-lifted, half pulled him out.

"Can you stand?"

Verne said, "Nothing . . . serious." He groaned and tried to grin. "Get Barb out. I'll crawl into your back seat and—" He groaned again. "Just—rest. Woe! My elbow! My damned leg, too!"

Adam reached toward me across Verne's empty seat. His face looked white and drawn.

"Slide across to me, darling, if you can. And don't jiggle the car. Just move slowly."

I did as he suggested, slid across the seat, out of the car, into his arms. As he was helping me to his car, we heard a siren and saw the lights of a California Highway Patrol car approaching around a curve in the highway.

Thank God we had Adam with us! Verne and I were not badly hurt, physically, but we were nervous wrecks and almost incoherent. Adam, whose presence I didn't question, managed to give all the immediate facts required by the patrol. He had seen the efforts of the Volkswagen to drive us over on the shoulder of the highway, though the car was too far away for him to get the license.

"Pretty stupid trick," he pointed out, "because a car as light as that could be demolished by a bigger car. But whatever the fool's aim, or the chance he took, it nearly worked. These kids came close to going over the side."

They had already put through a radio call to stop the black Volkswagen, but they weren't too optimistic.

"Must be a hundred of them on this highway alone tonight."

At Verne's anxious insistence, Adam arranged for his car to be delivered to the Museum exhibit as soon as possible. Everyone wanted to deliver Verne and me to the hospital at Auburn, but we protested with as much vigor as we could scrape up. Adam compromised by driving us to an emergency office in Colfax which was nearer, and after we were patched up with Band-aids, adhesive and aspirin, we were permitted to go, on the promise that we would get treatment in San Francisco.

Verne went to sleep in the back seat, but I had a bad case of shivers which couldn't be conquered even by the warm, muscular cushion of Adam's arm. But I loved his company, his presence, so much, I banished my suspicions of him for those hours it took to reach San Francisco.

Having passed Sacramento and eventually, Vellejo, we headed southbound onto the Carquinez Bridge. The toll booths reminded me of my trip with Verne in the other direction, and our discoveries in Reno.

"It was just one succession of shocks," I excused myself for my recent nervousness.

"I know, darling. I know. It was good of you to go and identify your father. It must have been very hard for you. I had already done so."

"You!"

"I can read, too. I saw the local paper."

I was really too tired to be angry, reserving that and all further thoughts of the ghastly business for tomorrow when I could concentrate.

Adam drove me to the hotel first, insisting that he would drive me out to the hospital for a checkup in the morning, which wasn't too far away. It was already past three A.M. I agreed, because I was too tired to do anything else. He left the mildly curious Verne in the car and took me to my suite, where I was not too tired to return his embrace and his kiss. Even in that hectic night I could tell that he was reluctant to leave, but we both mentioned poor, patient Verne at the same time and he left.

I went to sleep surprisingly fast after a brief but comforting bath to relax me. It was not until past noon the next day that I awoke to the buzz of the phone and found Adam apologizing for waking me.

"How do you feel?"

I had a slight headache and my muscles felt pulled and hauled, but I could honestly say I was reasonably myself.

"Except for a million questions. What on earth

were you doing in Reno? You didn't . . . make any trouble, did you?"

"If you mean, did I have Tom Tracey arrested, no. I had a little talk with him just after Verne left him with your money. I didn't find out what I wanted to know, but I'm progressing. I won't bother you with business right now. I'm coming by to take you for a checkup."

"I'm all right," I insisted but it was perfectly useless. In answer to my anxious questions about the dead Thomas Tracey, he said that Mr. Cortapassi had gone up to see to the return of the dead man and the funeral would be here in San Francisco on Monday. I knew that I had to see the Cortapassis, that Thomas Tracey was part of my life, whether he was my father or not, but I didn't tell Adam. He had his secrets. I had mine.

I dressed and waited for Adam, armed with several questions he still hadn't answered. I ate nothing because I wasn't sure what kind of examination I would be put through at the hospital. While we were driving out to the rambling hospital impressively perched on the steep slope of Geary Street, I asked Adam, "How did Thomas Tracey get to Reno? How did he get down the embankment into the river?"

"I wish I knew," he said grimly. He put his arm around me and ordered me, "Don't think about it. We'll have you out of the woods in a day or two,

I'm sure of it. Meanwhile, I'm going to keep you safe. No more near-misses. And another thing. We're going to get rid of that new will of yours. It's my belief none of this would be going on, you'd be in no danger, if you hadn't signed that will."

I was more at sea than ever, but I meekly agreed. Obviously, he still thought Tom Tracey was a phony, but I wasn't sure of anything.

"Guess who's at the hospital for a stay—short, we hope." He smiled but was clearly sympathetic, which pleased me.

"Not poor Verne Chandragar!"

"Oddly enough, it's his leg. The tibia. Simple, neat break, and the poor devil didn't feel a thing until I took him out here to be examined."

I told him about Verne's fall down the steps of the exhibit and he agreed that the break may have occurred then. He remarked, "It's an odd sort of accident, that business at the exhibit. The kid doesn't strike me as the clumsy sort."

"He's not. He fell over a thread. I had gone up to talk to him and he went down to ask his mother something . . ."

"You had gone up?"

I nodded. "I know. It could've been me. I think it was meant to be me." I took a deep breath. "I think it may have been the person in the black Volkswagen. Somebody is bound and determined to get rid of me. Or maybe Verne."

"Verne!" He laughed, then reconsidered and admitted I had a point there. "But he's safe in the hospital. It's you we've got to look out for the next few days. Maybe we can lock you into a room there until we get everything ironed out."

"Not on your life."

"We'll see," was all he would say to that.

But after my checkup, it was I who had the last word. I was perfectly all right. No bad aftereffects except a certain nervousness which Adam's doctor assured me was natural in the circumstances.

"You've got a fine, healthy young lady there, McKendrick. Hold onto her," was how the doctor put it.

Adam gave me a quick side-glance, a little embarrassed and anxious, I thought. But I smiled what I hoped was my *Mona Lisa* smile, and did not contradict the doctor. We went to visit Verne who was in an extremely agitated state until we explained that his doctor bills and hospital bills would all be paid.

"—and my repairs to old Betsy? She's a pretty good wagon."

"And the repairs to old Betsy," I added.

He relaxed in no time. In fact, he was full of suggestions. "First off, would it help you and the investigation if I told you I'm almost positive that was a California license on the black bug?"

I said, "But we were already in California when

it happened. It stands to reason it was a California license."

"Then it eliminates those Vegas guys Tom was talking about. Ma said they had a Nevada license, natch."

"Nevertheless," Adam put in, "it helps. Thank you."

"Ma's coming to see me soon as she can get off the box office. I don't suppose you could make me the loan of some folding money."

"So she can buy you some flowers?" I asked caustically, but then I laughed, and he grinned sheepishly.

"Well . . . there's always things you can do with folding money. Even in here."

In the end I left him his folding money. He had no false pride, and he wasn't a hypocrite. He took it with pleasure and reminded me as Adam and I were leaving, "You kind of owe it to me, seeing we never had a decent meal on that whole trip to Reno and back."

"Very true," I agreed gravely. I kissed him on the forehead and he beamed, which pleased me very much. On the way out I told Adam, "We must be about the same age, but he makes me feel like his mother. He may be a bit of a sponger, but I like him."

Adam surprised me by taking my hand and touching it to his lips. "So do I. Just as long as you don't like him too much."

After we both ate a belated lunch, he took me back to the hotel where late Saturday crowds were beginning to disperse to their favorite restaurants for the usual Saturday night festivities. I was suddenly very tired, and since I would be going to dinner with Adam at eight-thirty, I decided I wanted to be more than just a strained, nervous female full of questions and quick glances over my shoulder. I would take it easy, rest, try and calm down, be at my best for Adam. Make it hard for him to turn back to those widows and divorcees who were his chief clients.

But when he had gone, and I lay down and tried to close my eyes, I found myself buzzing with questions. Adam had promised that the mysteries around me might be solved and settled, the danger ended, but I couldn't help wondering meanwhile what the solution could be. I must have gone off to sleep eventually because when I awoke it was dusk. The telephone buzzed shortly after and for a few seconds I couldn't remember where I was. I blinked and felt for the phone.

It was Rose Cortapassi. She was firm, polite, and aloof. I understood why, and I could hardly blame her. She probably thought I was in some way responsible for the pitiful, even tragic death of their Thomas Tracey.

"Miss Tracey . . ." The old-fashioned, familiar and warm "Barbara-Jane" was gone and the loss hurt me surprisingly. "I tried to call you earlier, but you were not in."

"No. I was at the hospital." I couldn't resist that.

She was obviously shaken out of her frigid and disapproving calm. "You—you have been ill?"

"Not really. But some character on the highway tried to kill us, Mr. Chandragar and me, last night. I wasn't hurt. Just shaken up a little. But Mr. Chandragar's leg was broken."

"I see. I'm very sorry. Miss Tracey, I didn't intend to intrude, but I thought you might like to know that your father's funeral is set for two o'clock Monday afternoon at the Godeau Funeral Parlor on Van Ness Avenue. The burial—unless you have some objection—will be in the Catholic Cemetery at Colma. Holy Cross."

I was shaken by the news. It gave me a sudden little stab of anguish, as if my own father were to be buried, and I hadn't ever really known him.

"Thank you. I did want to know."

"Then I think that is all we have to say. Goodbye."

I was panicked. What if that poor man was my father? He had tried so hard to offer me love, a little attention, a father's natural interest. Now, he was gone forever.

"No! Please, wait! Mrs. Cortapassi, yesterday morning you mentioned some snapshots my—he took a long time ago. I wonder if I could see them."

She was clearly moved by my request.

"If you like. When would be convenient? Thomas had some little souvenirs of the old days. We've got them together in an old valise that Thomas brought when he moved in. There isn't much, I'm afraid."

I felt the prick of tears behind my eyes and cleared my throat before I was able to say, "I'd like to see them. As soon as possible."

She started to say something, spoke to Alfredo Cortapassi in the background, then suggested, "If you could come over now, we would appreciate it. The whole business of Thomas' trip to Reno is so incredible. You might tell us how it happened, if you would be so good. Alfredo has just returned from Reno. He was very upset. We understand nothing. Nothing!"

"Of course." A little dazed at the suddenness of this, I looked around at the electric clock on the night stand. It was 5:41 P.M. I had time to get over to the Cortapassis' and back before my date with Adam. Even better, I could dress now for the date and make quite sure of being ready when Adam came for me.

I showered and dressed and hurried out to get a taxi. I had become so used to the terrors of being followed for no accountable reason, by no identifiable people, that I kept looking anxiously out the rear window, much to the uneasiness of the cab driver.

"You in trouble, lady? I don't want any hassles with the fuzz."

I laughed abruptly. "It's nothing like that. But I've been followed lately, and I don't like it."

He looked in the mirror and whistled. "I can see why you're followed. Who is it? Husband? Boyfriend?"

"No," I said. "I don't really know who it is."

"Nothing to worry about now, anyway."

At least there was that for comfort.

We reached the Cortapassi house just before the foggy dark. Everything was different from that other visit with Adam. Then there had been their friendship and trust in me. Now, Mrs. Cortapassi was absolutely and flawlessly polite, but I knew she despised me and somehow associated me with the death of Thomas Tracey. Alfredo, however, was his old warm, emotional self. He embraced me, weeping, and repeated as I returned his hug, "My poor little one. You came all this way out west to find your Papa and he goes. No sense to it. Cruel. It was a cruel thing to do to you."

"Yes, it was, sir. Even more cruel to him. And it was deliberately done, I am sure. Someone killed him." Over her shoulder I saw Rose's face. There was a glitter in her dark eyes and her face thawed a little.

"You think that; do you?"

"I think he was tricked into going up to Reno. But I don't know how or why."

She nodded. "He was not well. He could not go that far unaided. But you are right. I would swear it. He was murdered. Maybe by that man in Reno. The one Mr. McKendrick says is the false Thomas Tracey."

I ignored that. I didn't want to think about it.

"You said you had snapshots and things belonging to Thomas Tracey."

"But Rose, my dearest one, can we find a little glass of that good wine, or better—the Ouzo, to warm our young friend as we look over the souvenirs of poor Thomas?" He got out a huge handkerchief and wiped his eyes. It was clear to me that his feeling for his old friend was utterly sincere. I hoped so. Everyone else seemed to have failed their Thomas Tracey, except the two goodhearted people here.

I told Mrs. Cortapassi not to trouble herself about the wine but she took it out, explained that it was not an Italian wine but Greek and that it would "cheer us all a little, perhaps." As she poured the Ouzo into liqueur glasses, I could smell the succulent odor of manicotti heating. It reminded me suddenly of that pleasant evening so short a time ago when Adam and I came to eat dinner with the Cortapassis and the man who tried so hard to be my father.

I was glad when they started out with me to the little cottage behind the garage. Even on this foggy night, the simple room with its studio couch, and the tiny bathroom with toilet, overhead flush box, and inadequate shower, all looked cozy and comfortable. The only sad thing was the old-fashioned, rust-colored valise on the couch. Alfredo went over and started to open it. The hasps stuck a little.

Suddenly I was struck by the vision of a little girl sitting cross-legged on the floor of Mother's apartment on Nob Hill, laboriously sewing something into the lining of a rust-colored valise. I cried out, startling myself as well as Mr. and Mrs. Cortapassi.

"Put your hands on the two ends and pull it open! And then look at the lining. The very center."

Alfredo did so. "Ah! Clever! Just a little pressure in the right places. So. And then what is this about a lining? It is very worn—what is it called, *cara mia?*"

"Threadbare." But she was not looking at the valise. She was staring at me and there was hope in her eyes.

"Yes. Threadbare like you say." Alfredo ran his fingers over what was left of the lining. He frowned a little. Clearly, he found nothing unexpected.

"Try this side," I suggested anxiously. Without

waiting for his discovery, Rose and I rushed to kneel before the valise and we all saw what remained of the initials at the same time. With a flamboyant orange embroidery thread I had once, long ago, created a monogram for Father on the heavy but now well-worn lining: T.M.T. The final "T" was gone but one "T" and "M" were still partly visible. They had been very wobbly when I first worked them, but I cried when I saw them now and what they stood for. All the years gone by and Father had never gotten rid of that shabby old valise and his daughter's childish work.

"Here, you will be interested in these funny pictures, little one." Alfredo took them out in an old, plain dime-store envelope and peeked into the envelope.

But it took Rose and me a little longer to get over the initials.

Alfredo looked from one to the other of us and sniffed mightily. "Now, now . . . do not cry, little ones . . . my two little ones."

I didn't need to look at the old black and white snapshots Father had taken with his Eastman bellows Kodak to prove what I already knew, but the memories of my infancy and childhood all came back with the sight of those pictures. There was one close shot especially of Father holding me up, showing me off, and I saw his left hand.

"Look. The spot just below his wrist. I thought it was a liver spot that came with his illness—your

Thomas Tracey, I mean. But I remember now. It was a kind of freckle. I remember!"

Rose nodded. I was terribly touched to see her blink and look away quickly.

I began to talk fast while borrowing Alfredo's handkerchief. "Adam and Mr. Rivercombe were right. They were sent the wrong set of prints and the Cortapassis' Thomas Tracey is—was Father all the time. If only I'd listened to Adam and not to my stupid, idiotic intuitions!"

"Don't cry!" poor Alfredo kept exclaiming, first to me and then to the heretofore imperturbable Rose.

But how had Father—this father of mine—known about my elevator accident in Madrid? There was this one bond between him and the false Thomas Tracey, the one I had so recklessly called *my* Tom Tracey. Would I ever know the truth of that?

Neither of the Cortapassis could help me there. They had never heard Father discuss my fear of heights, or the accident. We were all too emotional to discuss Father any more that evening, and it was almost with relief that I looked at my watch and discovered it was five minutes after eight and I would have only twenty-five minutes to get back for my dinner date with Adam.

I called a taxi and said good night to the Cortapassis. Mrs. Cortapassi stayed behind to put away Father's things until we could all examine them tomorrow—we hoped—with drier eyes. Alfredo walked out to the steps with me and then, when I hugged and said good night to him, he buried his face in his handkerchief again and wiped his eyes. I hurried down through the fog to the dim outline of the taxi.

I was very close, halfway across the sidewalk, before I realized this was not a taxi at all, but a sedan the color of a local cab. The driver got out. I don't remember how it happened, or why I didn't see anything, a face, arms, a weapon, anything. But the world seemed to fall on me and the darkness was complete.

CHAPTER 14

"What I need is an aspirin. No, two aspirins!" I told myself before I painfully opened my eyes.

. . . Of course! I'm on my way to Le Havre on the *France*. Or did I choose the *Elizabeth II* for this voyage? But what a cramped bed in this cabin!

I seemed to be in a lower berth. It was dark and for some reason my hands were both numb. Had I been sleeping on my hands somehow? Even without my hands, though, I knew there was an upper bunk overhead. Then, as my eyes became accustomed to the interior, I realized the faint blue-black light came from the porthole. From the starlit Atlantic sea and sky, undoubtedly. What was I doing in a cabin with an upper bunk? I hadn't shared a stateroom since I went to Europe one summer with my senior class from the select girls' school favored by Mother.

The cobwebs in my head cleared gradually. I tried to raise my arm to press it against my forehead in one of those useless gestures people make when they want to push back a headache. I couldn't move my arms. No. It was my hands. My arms moved. The muscles tightened, struggled to free those hands. At last, as my eyes began to make out the silhouettes of articles in the cabin, I realized my wrists were tied. Not too securely. Someone had been in a hurry. But one wrist was tied to the edge of the bunk and the other to the inner side of the springs. I found I could actually move my right wrist when I forced my muscles to react.

. . . Am I dreaming? I must be having a nightmare and imagining I am a prisoner . . .

But I could feel the ship moving under my body, listing badly, first to one side, then the other. No stabilizers on this crate. And no air-conditioning, either. It was stifling in here. And noisy. Grinding, gritty noises.

Even in a dream I wasn't going to lie here with my hands tied. My fingers were beginning to feel heavy and cold as ice. Which was weird, because already the heat in the cabin was making me cough. I twisted my right wrist until it was raw.

But the cords were loosening. I finally made an extra effort and sat up. I began to work on the cord with my teeth. It was a strong but slippery clothesline and whoever had tied me up had been unable to stop the slipping of the knot. The knot slipped easily and one hand was free.

By the time I got my left hand loose, I was coughing so much I could hardly breathe. The heat in here was frightful. I shook my hands frantically to get rid of that awful numbness. The pain of returning circulation was so biting, it at least served to tell me I was no longer dreaming. The cabin wall was warm, but when I stepped groggily onto the cabin floor and stumbled over to the porthole I found I couldn't touch the wall around the porthole. It was hot as an oven grill. Everything was intensely real.

I was in the *Morro Castle* exhibit. Were the simulated fire and the smoke meant simply to frighten me? Hardly. Not when combined with the lump on my head that still made me wince, and the clothesline that told me plainly enough that my unseen enemy had succeeded at last.

I ignored the headache, the coughing, the nasty stabbing pain of returning life to my fingers, and I rushed to the cabin door. I half-expected it to be locked, and I rattled the lock noisily at first, then frantically. I had some sort of idea that the lock would be old and I could force it. I kicked at it. I became hysterical for a few minutes, yelling and screaming, until I began to hear the grind of the machinery, wheels, cogs, some oiled, some rusty and screeching, all of them louder than my voice. Somebody must be getting an enormous kick out of this. I crossed the cabin, trying not to let panic destroy my common sense, and tried to open the porthole. It was nailed shut. Whether for my benefit alone or to scare the usual customers, I didn't know.

I banged on the glass with my fists. It must have been remarkably thick, not giving a fraction under my onslaught. But the cabin was lighter now, thanks to the clever "fire effects" outside, the glow apparently coming from below the porthole. Lights and reflectors, no doubt.

Suddenly, my tormentor moved too close to the edge of the floor above the cabin's ceiling. I saw his silhouette hunched over to peer down at the porthole and doubtless my face, scarlet in the light from the fake flames.

Chato.

Well, I knew that. Who else could work this devilish machinery so skillfully? But he wasn't the brain behind all this. He may have killed Thomas Tracey, my father. And he may have tried to promote those other disasters. But he wasn't the person who had told the two Tom Traceys that secret which no one could know about me. The business of the elevator crash. Chato wasn't the real brain, merely the hand.

I backed away from the porthole. I didn't want to feed Chato's malicious satisfaction.

All the effects were so real in this horrible exhibit that I began to imagine I smelled wood burning. The acrid, sickening stench that means destruction. A peculiarly hideous death. I rushed over to the porthole again. Smoke had begun to seep in near the cabin floor, little snakes spiraling upward into my lungs. I stood on tiptoe, feeling the heat through my shoes but trying to see the floor below the porthole. Those were not effect lights. They were real flames.

I ran around in there like a rat in a cage, looking for a piece of furniture, a weapon with which to beat down the door. I knew I was screaming but I couldn't seem to stop myself. Every piece of furniture, the bunks, the dressing table, everything was built in.

Except the dressing table drawers. I tried to pull one out. I pulled and hauled, finally drew it out and banged repeatedly against the door with this unwieldy battering ram. I thought for a minute or two that it would give way. But the drawer broke first. I had a handful of kindling.

I had been terrified of the flames but it was the smoke that would get me first. I was to be roasted before I was grilled. . . .

I tried to tear off a piece of the spread on the bunk. It always looked easy in the movies, but I couldn't even start a tear in the heavy, woven cloth. I pulled the entire spread off, coughing so I thought my lungs would burst. I crawled up to the upper bunk, remembering my fear of heights, but knowing that if I could get up there I would postpone my death by the flames for an added few minutes. I wrapped myself in the spread. I began to have visions, odd snatches of memory:

Of Father's face when he put his fingers over the embroidered monogram on the valise long ago . . .

My awful dead, black feeling that day in 1952 when we got on the ferry boat, Mother and I, on our way across the Bay to the Southern Pacific train in Oakland, the train that would carry us to Chicago . . .

And long years later, in Madrid, getting into that glass elevator, the slow descent, the noises of cogs and wheels and snapping pulleys, and the sickening, breathtaking fall . . .

Then, one night in Chicago last year. Glenn Rivercombe talking to me gently after my mother's senseless death in that car. He had said he wanted so badly to marry her, but she always refused. And me saying, "You really want to know how I feel? Like the day in Madrid when that elevator fell, and we were all covered with blood and glass. I feel numb. That's how I feel!"

God!

I sat up in the bunk, wrapped in the spread and trying to breathe only through that cloth. I knew now the answer to everything that had happened, and I knew why it had been necessary for me to write that will.

But I wouldn't die! I wouldn't give in . . .

I began to scream again. I hit at the ceiling, cursing, yelling . . .

The noises seemed to drown out my voice. Terrible, thunderous noises. And a great knocking in my head, like hammers. No. Like axes on wood.

I couldn't believe it, even when the cabin door burst in. Even when Adam McKendrick plunged in, ridiculously surrounded by splintering wood and shrouded in smoke.

"Here! I'm here!" I croaked at him, a writhing bundle of cloth that he lifted off the upper bunk and carried out with barely my eyes and the top of my head sticking out.

But I did see Tom Tracey as we passed him and the arriving firemen in that central passage, now so smoke-filled it was hard to see him distinctly. He was grinning, though, as he saw me moving in Adam's arms.

I cried hoarsely, "It was Mr. Rivercombe. He always intended to marry Mother. When she died, he knew he wouldn't get our money if I found my father; so he found him first and he must have made a deal with—"

"I know, honey. Save your voice. Tom Tracey told me all about it. Murder is not his speed, he said; so he—never mind. We'll talk about it later."

So I wound up in the hospital near Verne Chandragar, after all, but though the doctors kept claiming my lungs might have been damaged by the smoke, I proved to them I still had plenty of lung power when I wanted to get out of the place.

After much pressure from me, Adam arranged for me to be released. But when we were saying good-bye to Verne, Adam reminded me, "There is still some messy business ahead. There will be the trials. This Chato, for instance." I shuddered. "He was pretty badly burned when he set fire to that *Morro Castle* exhibit, but he's made a full confession. As I understand it, the original deal was made between your friend Rivercombe and your phony Tom Tracey."

"Now, wait a minute," I said. "I'm not going to prosecute Tom Tracey, I don't care what they try to make me do. He helped you to save my life. And I like him."

"So do I," Verne put in. He had his leg hoisted up on pulleys and things, but he was less concerned about this than about Rivercombe's plot to produce a fake father who would inherit my estate when I met with an unfortunate "accident." Verne went on, "I've had my suspicions about old Tom for a long time. But I knew if Tom was in it, then

Chato and Mother must know, and I couldn't face stooling on Ma. She's so mad at Chato now for trying to kill me along with you on the highway the other night that she'll be a big help to the prosecution." He laughed drily. "How you like a thin little squirt like Chato maneuvering that black bug like that. You got to hand it to him."

"Thin and little!" I protested. "He was strong enough to hit my poor father—my real father—on the head in that little cottage and then drag him off to Reno and leave him in the . . . Well, you know."

Verne shrugged, but he wasn't nearly as bound up in the death of Thomas Tracey as I was. "Well, sure, but he did that to throw old Tom's Vegas buddies off the scent, so they'd think he was dead. And it worked two ways, as far as Chato was concerned. Tom would be the only one left for Rivercombe to use. He'd end up with your money, he and Ma."

"And Chato!"

Adam had been listening to us amateurs reconstruct the crime, but he said now, soberly, "Chato seems to have done the whole thing, cooperated with Rivercombe, for your mother's sake."

"Don't expect me to sympathize with Chato now. Tell us the straight of it, Adam. Please." I sat down on the side of Verne's bed, shaking him accidentally so that he yelped. I got up in a hurry and apologized, but Verne waved that aside.

"Yeah. Tell us what it's all about and who we root for."

"Besides you," I put in, giving Adam my best smile.

"Certainly not for me. I fell for Rivercombe's trumped-up evidence from the start. As nearly as we can piece it together, Rivercombe's firm is deeply into your estate. Or at any rate, Rivercombe himself has had his hand in your till since long before your mother died. They still haven't gotten any kind of confession from him, but it's only a matter of time, with the eyewitnesses, the testimony of the others. Anyway, they've got Rivercombe. When your mother died, and you started talking about finding your father, he knew he had to work fast. There was a Tom Tracey . . . Verne's mother's friend. Ideally suited. He may even have been your father. He still insists he is."

"No," I said. "I won't deny my real father again. I saw the things in that old valise. Besides, those fingerprints! You yourself said the prints from the Maritime Union—or the government—got mixed up. Or Rivercombe said they were mixed up. The two Thomas Traceys. All that. But no matter what happened—"

"Darling, there really are two Traceys. Or were. And they both have worked on the docks here and —in Thomas Tracey's case—in Hawaii. Verne's Tom Tracey may not have Michael as his middle name. Anyway, he knew about the other one. He even told Rivercombe and Chato. That gave Rivercombe the idea that if one Tom gave him trouble, he could fall back on the other one."

Verne asked sharply, "What kind of trouble?"

"Tom found out Rivercombe intended to have Barbara killed. Tom figured if he refused to allow it, Rivercombe would have to agree. But Rivercombe simply began to use the other Tracey. Or rather, Rivercombe convinced me the other Tracey was the real one. And he sent a couple of Las Vegas fingermen after Tom. That was when Chato stepped in. He had no way of knowing the Vegas men were sent by Rivercombe, but by killing Thomas Tracey, Chato eliminated the problem. Rivercombe would now have to deal with Leah Chandragar's Tom Tracey."

Utterly confused, I started to sit down again, then, remembering Verne's leg, got up hastily.

"Then I'll have to spend the rest of my life trying to trip up Tom Tracey on some minor details, just to prove he isn't my real father!"

Adam shook his head and took one of my hands, which was, as always, a great comfort.

"No, darling. I'm ninety per cent sure your father was that man at the Cortapassis' place. But there is this ten per cent chance that Verne's wily friend, old Tom, is your father. We'll know soon. I don't have to rely on Rivercombe's so-called evidence now. I'm checking myself. You can have this consolation, that both your 'fathers' cared about you, and neither would have agreed to your murder. If they agreed with Rivercombe to share whatever you gave them, or settled on them, it isn't the same thing as murder. But that will of yours clearly shows the scheme; since he would have full control of most of your estate upon your death."

Verne sighed. "I was kind of thinking I'd been the hero in this mess. After all, I got wounded. But from what old Barb tells me, you ploughed through hell and high water to rescue our fair heroine."

"There was no high water," Adam corrected him gravely. "And in a way, Tom saved her. He flew back to town, called Barbara, and since I was practically pacing the lobby, a friend of mine on the switchboard asked if he would speak to me. He did. I figured you had gone to see the Cortapassis about the funeral and those snapshots. I called them finally. It was Tom who knew where we should go after that. The museum was closed. 'OUT OF ORDER' the sign said."

"That's what Chato told Ma, that it was on the fritz. So he'd closed up and she had gone home. Then it was a snap, I guess, bringing old Barb to that damned Morro Castle cabin."

I began to shiver and laughed in order to throw off the terrible memories. "You know, I'm rather

glad I don't know for sure which father was mine. Maybe you'd better not find out. Because I'll still have one father. Is that all right, Adam darling?"

"I couldn't agree with you more." Then he grinnned and drew me to him. "Just as long as you agree to only one lover."

"Lover!"

"Husband!"

"That's better."